Gulf Harbour ER

From ER drama to bedroom desire!

Gulf Harbour Hospital has one of the top emergency departments in New Zealand, and their medical staff is second to none. The ER is never short on drama…and when the stakes are that high, pulse-raising desire is bound to follow.

Four medics soon find themselves just one delicious, tension-fueled moment away from taking things from the emergency room to the bedroom!

Hotshot surgeon Mason Ward barely looked back when he left six years ago. So, consultant Lauren can't believe it when he breezes into *her* emergency department looking for a job.

Read Lauren and Mason's story in
Tempted by the Rebel Surgeon

Can opposites really attract? ER doctor Kat Collins must answer exactly that when clinical nurse specialist Nash Grady pushes all her buttons…

Read Kat and Nash's story in
Breaking the Single Mom's Rules

Both available now!

Dear Reader,

In this second book in the Gulf Harbour ER duet, *Breaking the Single Mom's Rules*, we return to the ER for Nash's story. Senior nurse Nash Grady is such a delicious guy—laid-back, dedicated to his job and even more dedicated to his five-year-old daughter, Molly. He needed a heroine who would rattle him so hard she turned his world upside down!
Enter Doctor Kat Collins, stickler for the rules and single mom to Molly's new best friend, Lucy.

For their own reasons, Nash and Kat have sidelined their personal lives. But spending day after day working together provides ample opportunity for them to clash, and when they do, the sparks begin to fly.

Their journey to love is not only aided by the passion they just can't resist, but also by the friendship between their girls. All they have to do is be brave enough to imagine the blended family they could be and put their hearts on the line.

Love,

JC x

www.JCHarroway.com

BREAKING THE
SINGLE MOM'S RULES

JC HARROWAY

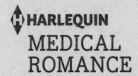

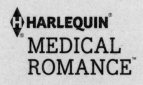

HARLEQUIN®
MEDICAL
ROMANCE™

Recycling programs
for this product may
not exist in your area.

ISBN-13: 978-1-335-73777-9

Breaking the Single Mom's Rules

Copyright © 2023 by JC Harroway

For questions and comments about the quality of this book,
please contact us at CustomerService@Harlequin.com.

Harlequin Enterprises ULC
22 Adelaide St. West, 41st Floor
Toronto, Ontario M5H 4E3, Canada
www.Harlequin.com

Printed in U.S.A.

Lifelong romance addict **JC Harroway** took a break from her career as a junior doctor to raise a family and found her calling as a Harlequin author instead. She now lives in New Zealand and finds that writing feeds her very real obsession with happy endings and the endorphin rush they create. You can follow her at jcharroway.com and on Facebook, Twitter and Instagram.

Books by JC Harroway

Harlequin Medical Romance

Gulf Harbour ER

Tempted by the Rebel Surgeon

Forbidden Fling with Dr. Right
How to Resist the Single Dad

Harlequin DARE

Forbidden to Touch
The Proposition
Bad Business
Bad Reputation
Bad Mistake
Bound to You
Tempting the Enemy

Visit the Author Profile page
at Harlequin.com for more titles.

To my sister, Lucy, an inspirational woman
and wonderful mother.

CHAPTER ONE

DR KAT COLLINS liked nothing better than a good to-do list and the accompanying sense of achievement when she crossed off each completed item. Sadly, when it came to patients, reaching the end of that list was impossible, as her first day in the emergency department at Gulf Harbour Hospital was proving.

Thanks to a boating accident out in Auckland's Waitematā Harbour, where many of the occupants hadn't been wearing life jackets, the ER had admitted three near-drowning victims. In addition, the city's largest sports stadium was host to an international rugby final, which brought in a constant stream of buoyant and boisterous casualties, many of them highly inebriated, loud and obnoxious. And, of course, neither of those events interrupted the everyday flow of people suffering from broken bones, chest pain or respiratory illnesses.

For Kat, dealing with the extensive backlog

of patients in both the resuscitation room and the minor injuries clinic helped to take her mind off her daughter, Lucy, who was currently partway through her first day at school. Heading for her next patient—a seventy-seven-year-old woman who had taken a fall at home that morning—Kat calculated that the new entrants' class of five-year-olds would be having morning tea right about then. A twinge of maternal worry tightened her chest. She loved her job, found the diversity and challenge of Accident and Emergency work varied and rewarding, but as a single parent working full-time she couldn't be in two places at once and was rarely free of parental guilt.

Would Lucy have made any friends? Did she like her lovely teacher, Mrs Alder? Would Kat need to answer the dreaded question about why Lucy's family only had a mum and no dad?

Swallowing down that pang of inadequacy that always accompanied thoughts of how she'd chosen the wrong man to father her beloved little girl, and that she not only carried all of the parental responsibility for Lucy but the financial responsibility too, Kat scanned her next patient's ambulance summary as she left the minor injuries area in search of Mrs Gibbs.

As she passed she smiled at one or two of the other staff, including her new boss and Head of

Department, Lauren Harvey. Her colleagues were so friendly and welcoming, making Kat feel like a valued member of the team.

For several minutes Kat scoured the department for her patient. Every corner of the chaotic ER was overflowing with people. Less urgent patients on stretchers even lined the corridors outside the ER's main treatment rooms, which was where Kat finally located Mrs Gibbs.

Kat approached the frail woman, noting that her eyes were closed, marvelling that she'd managed to nod off on a hard stretcher amid all of the noise and activity. Someone had covered her with a blanket, so all that was visible was her pale and gaunt face.

Kat checked the time on the admissions slip before waking the elderly woman, her frustration mounting to discover the poor lady had been waiting for over four hours to be seen. Kat winced, hating the unsatisfactory parts of her job. In an ideal world there would be enough beds and staff for all of the patients. But in reality limited staff and an unknown, ever-changing and potentially infinite waiting list of patients meant that delays were inevitable.

Gently resting a hand on Mrs Gibbs' shoulder, Kat woke her from a light snooze.

'Mrs Gibbs, sorry to startle you. I'm Dr Collins, one of the ER doctors.' She smiled her most reassuring smile, the one usually reserved for Lucy when she cried over a scraped knee or asked tricky questions about her father.

'Oh, that's okay, Doctor,' said Mrs Gibbs. 'I just closed my eyes for a second.' The woman struggled to sit upright.

Kat stilled her. 'Just relax for a few minutes while I ask you some questions.' Of course Kat would need to examine the patient, but she couldn't do that in a draughty corridor with no privacy.

'Thank you, dear.' Mrs Gibbs patted Kat's hand.

Her fingers were cold. Kat tucked the blanket up to the woman's chin, concealing her dissatisfaction with the system. She understood that no hospital was perfect, that accidents happened, placing enormous strain on already stretched resources, but she hated seeing vulnerable patients languishing in corridors. The sooner she could assess Mrs Gibbs and either admit her or send her home, the better.

'Tell me what's brought you in to see us today,' said Kat, taking the woman's radial pulse and reviewing the observations the paramedics had charted during the ambulance ride.

'Well, it's like I told that other lovely doctor,' Mrs Gibbs said. 'My feet got tangled around my neighbour's cat, you see, dear. He always comes to me first thing in the morning for breakfast, and I tripped over him and fell. Such a silly thing to do.'

Kat sympathised. As a cat owner herself, she could clearly envision the scene. But something about the story snagged her attention.

'What other doctor?' asked Kat, scrolling through the notes in case Mrs Gibbs had already been assessed by one of her ER colleagues.

'That one.' Mrs Gibbs pointed at someone over Kat's shoulder, her smile turning ever so slightly adoring.

Kat turned and spied Nash Grady, the department's clinical nurse specialist, who was currently taking blood from another patient further down the corridor.

'Oh, he's not a doctor,' Kat explained, relieved to clear up the simple mistake. 'That's Nash. He's our clinical nurse specialist.'

She'd met him briefly at the start of her shift, his easygoing, friendly smile causing a flood of unprecedented curiosity she'd assumed was long ago deceased, not for resuscitation, another casualty of her last relationship with Lucy's father, Henry. She just hoped that the smile she'd offered Nash in return had been less obvious than the one currently worn by Mrs Gibbs.

With a master's degree in nursing, Nash could assess patients and even prescribe treatment.

And as most of the ER staff wore scrubs it was no surprise that patients sometimes struggled to distinguish who was who, especially when their eyesight prevented them from clearly reading name badges. And with his tall and broad-chested physique and dark hair, Nash certainly carried off the scrubs spectacularly.

'That's the one.' Mrs Gibbs nodded, her expression dreamy. 'Lovely man. Very kind. He reminds me of my son.'

Observing the man who'd inspired Mrs Gibbs' devotion, Kat's rusty, battle-scarred libido stuttered to life. In that second, with both women staring his way, Nash looked up and locked eyes with Kat. A small smile twitched his lips, his expression tinged with a warmth and charm that made Kat suspicious. Closing her mouth, she hurriedly turned away.

'Let's move you somewhere private so I can examine you,' Kat said, mildly flustered from ogling the sexy nurse, who seemed to be friendly with everyone.

With her life full to the brim with her job, her daughter and the gratitude she owed to her parents, Kat had neither the time nor the inclination for work friends, especially when they came packaged as the department's charismatic, laid-back hottie.

She'd been fool enough to fall for Henry's

lure—the biggest mistake of her life. Not that she regretted the wonderful gift that was her darling Lucy, but for her daughter's sake she wished that she'd chosen a partner with a little more care, one interested in being more than a sperm donor.

Ignoring the sensation of heat on the back of her neck as she unlocked the wheels of the stretcher and pushed Mrs Gibbs past Nash, Kat reaffirmed that relationships and love were for the naive and deluded. And if her personal life lacked a certain sizzle, that was why romance novels and battery-operated toys existed.

She wheeled the cumbersome stretcher to the nearest freed-up examination cubicle, locking the wheels and drawing the privacy curtains. The medication chart showed that Nash had indeed seen Mrs Gibbs and prescribed some analgesia.

'I need to have a look at this sore leg of yours, Mrs Gibbs,' Kat said. 'Are you feeling comfortable enough for me to move you a little?'

Mrs Gibbs nodded. 'Yes, Doctor. The pain's not too bad now.'

'I'll examine your hip, and order an X-ray, just to be safe, although there might be a bit more of a wait, I'm afraid.'

Kat was about to raise the blanket from the patient's legs to begin her examination, when a hospital porter poked his head through the curtains.

'Is this Mrs Gibbs?' he said with a cheery smile that seemed to be the number one job requirement. 'I'm here to take you to the orthopaedic ward.'

Kat frowned. 'Hold on,' she said, confused. 'I haven't referred Mrs Gibbs to Orthopaedics. I haven't even examined her. She needs an X-ray and—'

The curtains swished aside once more and Nash appeared, flicking his bright reassuring smile Mrs Gibbs' way.

'Are you causing more trouble?' Nash asked the patient with a wink, clearly joking around in a way that made Mrs Gibbs giggle and Kat want to fan her face.

He moved to the patient's side opposite Kat and adjusted her pillows so she appeared more comfortable, his small considerations second nature in the way of all great nurses.

She'd bet he was universally adored by the patients.

'There seems to be some sort of mix-up,' Kat said, her stare swooping from Nash to the hospital porter, who was already raising the side of Mrs Gibbs' stretcher in preparation for wheeling her from the ER and up to Orthopaedics. A niggle of irritation sent prickles down Kat's spine. She was losing control of this consultation before it had even properly begun.

'Mix-up?' Nash asked, smiling down at Mrs Gibbs before levelling his gaze on Kat.

Her heart began to gallop now that she was trapped in the focus of the man responsible for the first pulse of attraction she'd experienced in over five years.

But her job was the only area in her life where she felt in control. The rest—being so thoroughly betrayed by Henry, being forced to raise Lucy alone, watching the consequences of her mistake unfold and affect the people she loved most—were circumstances that had been thrust upon her and therefore only added to her sense that she was doing things badly.

Swallowing the irrelevant thrill of excitement coursing through her body, she gripped the rail of the stretcher. 'I know it's my first day—' she directed her comments to Nash '—but I'm confused. The notes indicate that I'm the only doctor to see Mrs Gibbs.'

Nash shrugged, unlocking the wheel brakes and pushing the foot of the stretcher away from the wall. 'You *are* the only doctor to see Mrs Gibbs, but she's one of the lucky ones.' He gave Mrs Gibbs another wide smile. 'She'll be spending the night as a VIP guest in Orthopaedics.'

Kat scrabbled around for the missing punchline, her patience wearing thin. 'I haven't referred her to Orthopaedics.' Offering Nash a tight smile, she folded her arms. A mistake, because now she'd lost the game of stretcher tug-of-war.

'I know,' Nash said with a casual shrug and then addressed Mrs Gibbs as if the matter was decided. 'We've laid on Graham, the best porter in the whole hospital, to take you to Ward Twenty-Five, where they'll look after you like a queen or they'll have me to answer to, okay?'

'Thanks, dear.' Mrs Gibbs beamed, both her and Nash oblivious to the tension coiled around Kat like razor wire.

She strived to be good at her job, liked to do things by the book. If there was a different protocol to follow at this hospital she wanted to be informed. His laid-back charm, his rapport with the patients was all very well, but procedures and regulations helped to avoid mistakes.

With a stifled sigh of defeat, Kat watched the porter wheel the patient towards the lifts, throwing a 'Cheers, Grady' over his shoulder. Nash swished the curtains fully open and wiped Mrs Gibbs' name from the whiteboard on the wall, freeing the bay for the next patient.

'Hold on a second,' Kat said, following his rapid footfall down the corridor. She refused to be dismissed. 'We need to talk.'

What on earth was going on? What sort of a place had she come to work in? Were there no rules at all?

'Can't it wait?' Nash said without glancing her way. 'It's pretty crazy today and we all have lives we want to get home to at the end of our shifts.' He logged into the nearest computer and began flicking through some notes.

Kat was certain there would be steam coming out of her ears. 'I know how busy it is. I work here too, remember. Which is why I'd appreciate an explanation. I was about to examine that patient and send her to X-ray, if needed. I don't enjoy being professionally undermined.'

'She'll have her X-ray from the ward,' he said, his fingers rapidly typing. 'And she'll be much more comfortable there while she waits. I wasn't undermining you, just thinking about the patient.'

Because he still hadn't looked up from the screen, because he was acting as if it was okay to throw protocol out of the window as long as he flashed his dazzling smile, she employed her frostiest tone. 'So, who authorised her admission to Orthopaedics?'

Logging off the computer, he finally turned to face her, sparing her thirty seconds of his undivided attention.

'*I* authorised her admission, Dr Collins,' he said, his tone cool and clipped.

Momentarily distracted by his eyes, which were the colour of chestnuts flecked with gold, Kat reacted to the fact that his relaxed attitude seemed to be slipping.

'I realise that,' she said, annoyance now her overriding driver, 'but—'

He held up a hand, cutting her off. 'We have two more elderly ladies like Mrs Gibbs who have been waiting just as long, so can I suggest that, for now, we set aside our differences and do our jobs?'

Kat's jaw dropped. Insufferable man. She'd been trying to do her job when he'd muscled in and done things his own way.

Before she could argue further, he grabbed a stethoscope from the desk. 'If you still have a problem with my methods, once things have calmed down,' he said, backing away, leaving Kat in a scented cloud of his delicious aftershave, 'feel free to take it up with me later.'

Kat most definitely had a problem, but it was too late. He'd already turned his back on her.

'Welcome to Gulf Harbour, Dr Collins,' he threw over his shoulder.

All Kat could do was silently fume.

CHAPTER TWO

AT THE FIRST lull in the organised chaos that filled the ER that day, Nash Grady—or Grady as he was widely known since his army days— looked up from the notes he was making, unsurprised to find that the new registrar had come to settle their unfinished business.

'Dr Collins,' he said, acknowledging her presence while he typed up the suturing procedure he'd just completed on a drunken footy fan who'd fallen over and smacked his head on the pavement. All he wanted to do today was get through this horrendous shift, go home and hear all about his daughter Molly's first day at school.

But first he'd have to deal with Kat Collins.

'What can I do for you?' he went on, spinning his chair to face her. Dealing with her meant reining in the flare of attraction he'd experienced the minute she'd walked into the ER that morning.

Even gunning for him, her full mouth pinched with annoyance, those big blue eyes of hers narrowed, she was gorgeous. Not that it mattered. She could be the woman of his dreams and he still wouldn't be interested. He was a veteran of a failed marriage, a practically full-time single parent. That rarely left time to notice attractive women.

'I'd like to finish our conversation,' she said, jutting out her chin in confrontation. Showing him that she had no intention of being fobbed off a second time, she crossed her arms over her chest, a move that cinched in the waist of her scrub top and made the appealing outline of her figure more noticeable.

Grady sighed, mentally reviewing their earlier interaction. Yes, she was prickly and uptight and had already formed a pretty low opinion of him if the way she'd questioned his methods earlier was any indication. But perhaps he'd been a little short in return. He'd normally make a new member of staff feel welcome: give them a tour of the department, take them to the hospital cafeteria, chat about their previous experience and their expectations for their new position. But not only had it been a crazy morning, Kat Collins was far too distracting for his usual warm and welcoming meet and greet. She was an absolute bombshell. Tall, blonde, intelligent.

And, from the dressing-down he expected he was about to receive, she also took no nonsense.

'Okay, let's talk,' he said, standing. They were in the centre of the busy staff hub, a workspace away from patients dedicated to computer stations and the large whiteboard they used to list each patient in the department.

Kat Collins and her agenda was the last thing he needed when his day had already begun with his ex-wife, Carol, dropping in before breakfast. Her unannounced visits usually disrupted the calm he tried to maintain, but today there had also been an uncharacteristic flood of tears from Molly, who would only be appeased if Mummy joined them for the trip to school.

'Just so I'm clear on how you do things here,' Kat said, resuming their disagreement. 'You admitted Mrs Gibbs *without* a diagnosis and before she'd been seen by a doctor, is that right?'

'I did,' Grady said, trying his best to ignore the withering contempt in her voice. He prided himself on his integrity, always tried to do the right thing. That was how he'd ended up in a rushed marriage, one doomed to failure. He and Carol hadn't really known each other, nor had Carol been particularly interested in rectifying that situation.

But the reminder was timely. No matter how

many positive attributes this new doctor had, Molly was his number one priority.

'Why?' Kat asked, fisting her hands on her hips.

'Because I diagnosed what is most likely a fractured neck of femur. Because she'd been sitting in the cold corridor waiting to be seen for hours. Because I knew she'd be more comfortable waiting for an X-ray on the ward and I don't like to see patients suffering.'

He'd spent enough time in the ER with Molly as a patient to know how intolerable those wait times could be.

Thinking about his five-year-old daughter's health, his protective urges rose to the surface, the concern that he'd had to force down while he managed the morning's unexpected influx of patients reawakening. What if her upset this morning triggered an asthma attack at school? Would Carol's insistence that she be the one to pick Molly up that afternoon create more distress for their daughter, especially when Carol would once more disappear for an unknown period of time?

The only stability in Molly's life came from the calm routines he tried to maintain during his ex's prolonged and unpredictable absences, but Carol rarely thought about anyone other than herself, oblivious to the trail of drama she left behind.

'How do you know that your diagnosis was correct, Nash?' Kat asked, drawing his thoughts back to a matter that, as far as he was concerned, was resolved.

Her accusing tone needled him like a bee sting. He wasn't reckless. The army had taught him that sometimes you had to act on instinct, even if it deviated from the rulebook.

'I'm good at my job,' he stated simply. Although he'd learned during his marriage that trying your best, doing everything right, wasn't always enough.

'As the admitting doctor,' she continued, 'I'd planned to take a complete history, examine the patient and then order the relevant tests.'

Grady nodded, searching for the patience he was well known for. Hopefully Kat wasn't one of those doctors who believed that some roles could only be performed by members of her profession. A nurse's job wasn't confined to changing bed pans and taking temperatures, especially nurses with his qualifications.

'And had you done all of those things,' he said, keeping his voice even, fighting the urge to check his watch, 'I'm sure you'd have come to the same diagnosis as I did.'

Because he still had a list of jobs the length

of his arm to do before he could meet Carol and Molly back at his house, he headed for the treatment room, fully expecting Kat to follow.

'By the way—' he took a key from a collection worn around his neck on a lanyard and unlocked the treatment cupboard where all of the medications were stored '—most people around here call me Grady.'

It had been a long time since anyone had called him Nash. Even Carol had adopted Grady. He hated to admit that his first name sounded way too good on Kat's lips.

Kat huffed. 'Well, I dislike nicknames.'

'Fair enough.' He grinned to himself as he selected two vials of intravenous antibiotics from the cupboard before relocking it. 'Although it's not a nickname. It's a hangover from my army medic days that just stuck.'

Sometimes he missed the camaraderie of the army, not that he regretted leaving to be more of a family man. Being Molly's father was more fulfilling than any job in the world. He'd wanted stability for his daughter, to be there for dinner and bedtime, to read stories and provide cuddles. And given Carol's general dissatisfaction with parenthood, his decision had worked out for the best.

Focused on what he was doing, he injected sterile saline into a vial of antibiotics and shook it to dissolve the powder into a solution, all the while conscious of Kat's warm scent—whimsical floral accents and woman. Not that he'd ever met a woman less whimsical than Kat Collins. She was practically ironing board straight, the biro, pen torch and notebook neatly regimented in the top pocket of her scrubs. Her golden hair was pulled back into a tight ponytail, not one single strand out of place. Even the pale freckles dotting her nose and cheeks were uniform and symmetrical. He'd bet his life's savings that she used hospital corners to make her bed at home.

'Well, I don't know how they do things in the army,' she said, tossing her hair over one shoulder, 'but there are protocols in hospitals—protocols *I* prefer to follow.'

Smiling because his nonchalance seemed to ruffle her feathers, Grady nodded. 'You are absolutely right, there are protocols. I know because I helped to write them, despite only being a nurse.'

Was she for real, throwing the rulebook in his face? He wasn't some inexperienced student. He'd worked in the medical field longer than her, earned his master's degree. He'd been deployed overseas as an army medic, treated wounded colleagues and civilians before taking the position at Gulf Harbour when Carol had discovered she was pregnant.

Kat sighed as if she were dealing with a small, misbehaving child. 'I wasn't implying that you're not qualified. But in my experience patient referrals are made by medical staff, *after* a diagnosis is made and all relevant tests have been ordered.'

She tilted her chin triumphantly.

He reached past her to dispose of the needle in the sharps bin, caught her quick inhale of breath when the move brought them closer than before. Was she attracted to him too? Well, wouldn't that be highly inconvenient for a woman who probably made lists for fun.

'And in an ideal world,' he said, shoving the irrelevant thought aside, 'with ample time and resources, every case would be perfectly managed according to the rules and protocols, but sometimes it's better to be flexible.'

'Flexible?' She gaped as if he'd suggested handing each patient a textbook so they could treat themselves.

'That's right, it means adaptable,' Grady said, pointing out the obvious and noting how the flare of challenge lit her pretty eyes. 'Here at Gulf Harbour we occasionally use our intelligence and initiative and extensive clinical experience to dispense with strict protocol, especially at times of stress to the system and when we have elderly and frail patients waiting unacceptable lengths of time to be seen by busy doctors.'

Kat spluttered, actually spluttered with indignation.

Looking away from her full mouth, he breathed through his inclination to be unusually obstructive. Who was this doctor telling him how to do his job, how to run his department on her first day? Even if her reprimand was justified, he had a patient waiting for the antibiotics he'd just prepared and a meeting to attend before he could leave for the day. As it was, he'd be lucky if he had a chance to eat the apple he'd grabbed from home that morning, let alone to take a proper break.

As if sensing his imminent departure, Kat positioned herself in his path, literally blocking his escape. 'No disrespect, but—'

'Most disrespect begins with that disclaimer,' Grady said, interrupting. 'Just so you know.'

She ignored him. 'But aren't you, with your flexible methods and disregard for protocol, scared of missing something? Of making a mistake? You can't possibly know that your diagnosis is correct without an X-ray.'

He sighed, momentarily closing his eyes and dragging in a calming breath that was maddeningly laced with her scent. He'd chosen nursing as a career in order to help people. Sometimes that meant bending the rules in order to minimise suffering and keep the entire system working. Now this woman was more or less suggesting that he was deliberately putting patient safety at risk.

'She's probably had her X-ray by now,' he said, 'along with a nice warm, comfortable bed and some attention from the ward nurses, rather than occupying a hard ER stretcher in a draughty corridor, where no one really has time to chat to her about her grandkids.'

Hesitation flickered across Kat's face. It gave him pause. Like him, she was fighting for the best patient outcome. They just had different ways of doing things.

Then, as if deciding the argument was still worth winning regardless of logic, she narrowed her stare. 'Yes, but rules are not bendable. You should have waited for me to confirm the diagnosis.'

Grady stepped closer, still trapped by her stubborn presence in the doorway, still distracted by the way she looked at him while she tore off a few strips, still determined that her attractiveness and what was clearly the most chemistry he'd experienced in a long time could be ignored.

'Rules can be bendable if you know what you're doing.' He stared, refusing to acknowledge how her breasts rose into his line of vision with her rapid breaths. 'And, as per the remit of my role, I took clinical history. That's how I found out that Mrs Gibbs has osteoporosis, a risk factor for fractures.'

She opened her mouth to argue but he ploughed on, frustratingly more aware of her femininity than ever. 'I also examined her and guess what? Her right leg was shortened and externally rotated, indicating a likely fractured neck of femur.'

Grady could almost see steam coming out of her ears, she was so wound up. But if she thought she could swan into the ER and start waving her rulebook around or make him jump through her hoops she could think again. It didn't matter how stunning she was or how much she stirred his libido, or how fascinating and energising he found her challenge.

He'd once tried everything in his power to please Carol, but nothing he'd done had been good enough. He'd vowed to never make the same error again. He had nothing to prove to this woman.

'So, as you can see, Dr Collins, I made a diagnosis and ordered an X-ray for confirmation. I know from my extensive past experience seeing hundreds of similar cases that my diagnosis was likely correct—by the way, she's the fourth patient this week alone with the same presentation. But as it's your first day here I'll let your slightly patronising lecture on following the rules as you see them slide, just this once.'

But Kat wasn't ready to back down.

'So doing the right thing is for the rest of us, not you?' she volleyed. 'You can just do what you like, regardless of how it might affect others.'

'Well, that's not at all insulting,' he said. 'Look, I'm here to do my job to the best of my abilities.' Keeping his anger at bay, he held his ground. 'That includes doing everything in my power to keep patients like Mrs Gibbs comfortable and moving through the department.'

He agreed with Kat in principle, but sometimes there wasn't a nice clean-cut solution. He'd learned that the hard way during his rocky marriage, was still learning the lesson every time Carol threw him a curveball, just like today, irrespective of what might be best for Molly.

Aware that he'd allowed this woman to rile him up until his pulse was throbbing at his temples, he took a calming breath. 'Your concern for my methods is noted. Thank you for bringing your opinions to my attention. Now, if you'll excuse me, I have other patients to help, and I'm sure you do too. Any further comments on my performance can be directed to our departmental head, your boss, Dr Lauren Harvey.'

He smiled. 'Enjoy the rest of your first day, Dr Collins.'

Shoving down the emotions, good and bad and downright inconvenient, that she'd roused in him, Grady left the treatment room. First thing tomorrow he'd rearrange his shifts so he and Kat spent as little time as possible working together. She might be beautiful, but clearly they had nothing in common.

No, Kat Collins was a complication Grady in no way needed in his life.

CHAPTER THREE

RELIEVED TO FIND a parking space, Kat parked her car on a residential side street a short walk from Harbour View Primary School. She couldn't be late for pick-up on Lucy's first day. Nor could she turn up still horribly distracted by her frustrating altercation with Nash Grady.

Bendable rules… Huh! Who did he think he was?

Realising that a large part of her animosity was aimed at Henry, another man who thought he could do whatever he liked without a care for the consequences, Kat tried to take a few calming breaths before she left the car.

Most of her woes circled back to Henry. Just like he was currently missing his daughter's first day at school, her ex had also missed out on every other important milestone of Lucy's life: her birth, first tooth, five consecutive birthdays and Christmases. Hurt and humiliated by his rejection, at first Kat had tried to think of his choice not to be in his daughter's life *his* loss. Except around the time Lucy was old enough to understand the difference between a mummy and a daddy, Kat had begun to resent Henry anew. His selfish rejection, his continued absence impacted not only Kat, who was raising Lucy alone, but also Kat's parents, who regularly stepped up to help out with childcare so Kat could work, despite her father's stroke. And, most importantly of all, his desertion affected Lucy and would for the rest of her life.

With her stomach wound in a familiar knot of anger and self-recrimination, Kat grabbed her bag and locked up the car, hurrying along the street. Her fears that her beautiful daughter had been somehow irretrievably disadvantaged by Kat's disastrous taste in men were a constant niggle in the back of her mind, one of the reasons she'd been so off-kilter today.

Six years ago, blinded by what she'd thought was love but what she now considered naiveté, she'd chosen the wrong man. A man who, when she'd told him she was pregnant, had casually informed her that fatherhood was *not for him*, as if creating a life was like a jar of tart marmalade he'd tried once but wouldn't buy again, and that he wanted no part in Kat's life or the life of his child.

No wonder she'd allowed Nash and his laid-back charm and winning good looks to burrow so far under her skin. Thanks to Henry, Kat had an enduring distrust of ridiculously attractive men, and Nash Grady fitted the description like a hand in a latex surgical glove.

Pushing through the school gate, Kat forced a smile onto her face and tried not to ruminate on what she considered her biggest mistake.

Bad enough that she'd fallen in love with the most unreliable man on the planet, her penance hadn't ended with Henry's rejection. Foolishly grieving his loss and ashamed that she'd been stupid enough to fall for his superficial veneer in the first place, Kat had returned to New Zealand, her overseas working holiday in the UK cut short. She'd been forced to move back in with her supportive parents. Her pregnancy had been complicated by hyperemesis gravidarum, the severe form of morning sickness, in the first trimester, and she'd developed pre-eclampsia in the third trimester. Kat was still convinced that the stress of having her home, of watching his only daughter go through such a difficult pregnancy had contributed to her father's stroke.

Checking her phone, Kat fired him a quick text, asking how he was going with the daily crossword they'd begun to do together as part of his rehabilitation after his stroke. It helped with his memory and language skills and boosted his confidence.

If only it could ease a fraction of her guilt.

Kat arrived outside Lucy's classroom just as the school bell sounded. She loitered with a group of other nervous-looking parents, all eyes focused on the classroom door in anticipation. Seconds later, accompanied by their teacher, a steady stream of cute five-year-olds appeared, their new uniforms baggy with growing room and their backpacks dwarfing their small frames.

'Mummy!' Lucy cried, trotting towards Kat with an enormous grin on her angelic face.

Kat exhaled a relieved breath at the sight of her daughter's cheery smile.

She wanted to call Henry right now and yell, *See? Despite you carelessly throwing me away like rubbish, calling me irresponsible and selfish, there's nothing wrong with me. I'm a good mother and your daughter is happy and well-adjusted.*

Not that he deserved to know anything about the amazing child they'd made together.

Lucy held what looked like a first reading book in one hand and a fellow classmate—a freckled little girl with skewwhiff pigtails and huge dark eyes—by the other hand.

Kat caught the eye of Mrs Alder, who was

speaking to one of the other parents nearby. The teacher logged Kat's presence with an efficient nod.

Kat crouched down, accepting the book Lucy thrust her way.

'That's my reading book,' her daughter said, full of importance. 'Molly got one too. Molly is my new friend. We're reading partners.'

The girls looked at each other and giggled as if they'd been friends since birth, their tightly clasped hands swinging between them.

A lump of gratitude the size of a watermelon lodged in Kat's throat. Lucy hadn't spent her first day sobbing or sitting alone in the corner or being teased for not having a father. Her brave, beautiful girl had made a lovely friend.

'Hello, Molly. It's nice to meet you.' Despite all of Kat's reservations that by giving her a father like Henry she'd ruined Lucy's life, surely this wonderful first day success meant that her daughter was going to be okay.

Kat eyed the nearby parents in search of one who might belong to Molly, hoping to foster the friendship and perhaps make a new friend herself, although she had little time for socialising. She'd spent every minute of the past five years working, helping out her parents or being a mother to the best of her abilities, which some days she feared were at best a B minus.

But not today. Today was an A plus day.

Today, she could shake off the doubts Henry's cruel rejection had embedded in her psyche.

Kat stood, tucking the reading book into the pocket of Lucy's backpack, in no hurry to leave since Molly was still unclaimed. Hating that her ex still had the potential to taint a brilliant moment of mother and daughter triumph, Kat busied her mind with imagined play dates and future sleepovers with Lucy's new-found friend. Trips to the beach and joint birthday parties. With a best friend at her side, maybe Lucy wouldn't notice that her family was different.

While the girls chatted and laughed, Kat checked the text from her father, her spirits lighter.

Everything felt better now that her worries for Lucy's first day had lessened. She could even reflect on her disagreement with Nash, acknowledge that he'd acted within his job description, even if she'd have handled things entirely differently.

Clearly, they had nothing in common. But perhaps next time they shared a shift she should apologise, clear the air.

Flushed with a new sense of achievement, Kat watched both girls perform some kind of funky dance to which only they knew the moves.

A glimpse of Henry in their daughter's facial

expression caught Kat off-guard, as it often did. How could a person not want anything to do with their own flesh and blood? Rejecting her she could handle, but his rejection of their child she'd never understand or forgive.

'Mummy...' Lucy said, drawing Kat away from the return of her dark thoughts. 'Molly says there's a park near here and she's going there with her mum after school. Can we go too?'

'Um...maybe,' Kat hedged, not wanting to commit to a firm *yes* until she'd met Molly's mother. 'Can you see your mum, Molly?' Kat asked now that the group of parents and kids left in the playground had thinned to a few stragglers.

Kat couldn't wait for ever. It was a school night. Her hectic first day had left her craving a home-cooked meal that she hadn't planned, a hot bath that would probably end up tepid once Lucy's ablutions had used up most of the hot water and an early night she had no chance of achieving because she still had study to do once she'd settled Lucy into bed.

But maybe she could bend the rules just this once in celebration of Lucy's momentous first day success.

Molly's smile switched to a small frown as she glanced around the playground. It was as if she'd forgotten to seek out her own parent in all the excitement of leaving class with her new friend. Her eyes rounded with uncertainty, her lip trembling.

Kat's stomach dropped. The last thing she wanted to do was to make someone else's child cry because she'd pointed out that their mother was late for pick-up. It happened. It could just as easily have been Kat if her boss, Lauren, hadn't found her five minutes before her shift ended and insisted on taking over the assessment of Kat's patient.

Despite Lauren's high expectations for her ER, despite not having a family of her own, Kat's boss was fair and supportive. Her only flaw seemed to be her longstanding friendship with Nash but, as Lucy and Molly had proved, everyone deserved a friend.

'Don't worry,' said Kat with an overly bright smile. 'She'll be here soon.' She didn't want the girls' first day to end in tears.

Molly's eyes shone. Not even Lucy could coax a smile. Kat was about to interrupt the teacher for support when Molly squealed excitedly and ran off.

Relieved, Kat grabbed Lucy's hand to stop her daughter chasing after her new best friend. Perhaps a trip to the park wasn't such a good idea. The five-year-olds had had a long day.

Emotions were bound to be fragile. Better to end on a high.

Hoping to manoeuvre Lucy to the car without too much fuss or begging, Kat pocketed her phone and turned away from the classroom. She wasn't looking where she was going, which was how she ended up colliding with a hard, delicious-smelling male chest.

'Oh, sorry,' she muttered, disentangling herself and shuffling aside.

'My fault, sorry,' the man said, one hand gripping Kat's arm as if to stop her falling to the ground and the other wrapped around Molly.

Kat's brain blinked off and on as she tried to compute what, or rather who, she was seeing.

Nash Grady was the owner of the deliciously buff chest. Nash Grady's aftershave was filling her senses and making her want to close her eyes on a dreamy sigh. Nash Grady was touching her arm, the tingles zapping along her nerve-endings reminding her that this was the most intimate touch she'd experienced in almost six long and sexually barren years.

Kat swallowed, her body ignoring every first impression she'd formed of her disagreeable colleague.

Seeing she was steady on her feet, Nash dropped his hand.

Kat rebounded from the loss of his warm

touch. Her legs felt insubstantial, her head swimming from the lingering scent of him: citrus and spice and the ocean breeze. Her breasts tingled where they'd briefly made contact with his muscular chest.

He was ignoring her now, instead soothing a sobbing Molly.

A sharp spike of envy all but swept Kat's feet from under her as she watched him stroke Molly's hair back from her tear-soaked face. He whispered reassurances into the little girl's temple, all of his focus on Molly, as if nothing else existed.

Pulling herself together as best she could with her raging lust hormones let loose, Kat tried to close her mouth, tried not to stare, to make her feet move. She didn't want him to witness the effect his touch had on her.

But before she could make the appropriate brain synapses fire Nash shot her an apologetic look, as if finally remembering his manners now that Molly's tears were mostly over.

'Are you okay?' he asked.

She must have bumped her head when she'd collided with him because the flicker of heat, an awareness that hadn't been there before, lingering in his stare couldn't be real.

Kat cleared her throat. 'Um…yes… Sorry, I didn't see you.' Oh, good, she'd not only body-slammed the only man in six years to jumpstart her libido, she'd also temporarily lost the power of intelligent speech. 'What are you doing here?'

As if recognising her for the first time, as if recalling their difference of opinion and how she'd as good as accused him of mismanaging a patient, his eyes hardened. 'I'm collecting Molly from school,' he said with perfect reasoning.

From her position snuggled into his chest, Molly turned red-rimmed eyes on Kat and Lucy. Kat took a second look at those eyes: the colour of chestnuts flecked with gold.

That was when Kat's brain began to work once more. Time stopped as reality dawned.

No, no, no. It couldn't be true. Fate wouldn't be that cruel to Lucy, even if it had no such compunctions for Kat's emotional welfare.

'Where's Mummy?' Molly asked, her lip trembling anew so Kat's heart lurched with empathy for Lucy's new friend.

Nash placed Molly on the ground as if she were a priceless work of art and gently cupped her face. 'I'm sorry, darling. She had to work. But that's lucky for me because I get to take my best girl to the park, right?'

Kat watched in wonder as Molly smile turned from hesitant to beaming. She threw her little arms around his neck. 'I love you, Daddy.' Even her eyes were closed in relieved bliss.

'I love you too.'

Accepting that the universe clearly hated her, Kat looked down at her feet, away from the sight of the kind of father-daughter moment that Lucy would never know. Typical that Molly's *daddy* was the one and only laid-back, rule-bending Nash Grady. Out of all the kids in Auckland, Lucy had chosen Molly Grady—the cute-as-a-button daughter of Kat's new work nemesis—as a friend.

And worse, despite the fact that she and Nash were destined never to see eye-to-eye, her body seemed to be having some sort of revolt, as if watching a man parent was the ultimate turn-on.

'You're Molly's dad,' she said, stating the obvious, her voice as flat as a week-old helium balloon. She owed it to Lucy to at least be polite. But there was no chance of the parental friendship she'd envisioned. Not with him.

'I am,' he confirmed, standing and taking Molly by the hand. His gaze sought Mrs Alder over Kat's shoulder and he mouthed the word *sorry*.

Now his lateness made sense. No doubt Nash applied the same flexibility to time as to protocol and rules.

'And who is this?' he asked, smiling down at Lucy. To his credit, his expression showed no sign of ill-will following their earlier disagreement.

'It seems our daughters are reading buddies,' Kat said, introducing her daughter, secretly fascinated by the attention he lavished on Molly. He might be casual about his timekeeping, but he and Molly obviously had a very close relationship. Lucy's closest male role model was Kat's father, where Molly had the real thing—an apparently doting father. Even if that father was the man who had ruined Kat's first day at Gulf Harbour, she couldn't deny that his attentiveness towards Molly made him twice as hot in Kat's book.

Good thing there was a wife in the picture.

'Hi, Lucy.' He smiled broadly at her daughter in a way that spoke directly to Kat's ovaries. She glanced at his left hand for a wedding ring, hoping its presence would kill what now appeared to be the first serious man crush she'd had since Henry.

There wasn't one. But it didn't matter. Her hormones would soon get the message that her life was full to the brim as it was, without a man, without sex. A couple more clashes of opinion with Nash would likely do the trick in killing the unwanted urges.

'Thanks for waiting with Molly,' Nash said,

his eyes meeting Kat's once more. 'You didn't need to.'

For the first time since they'd literally bumped into each other, Kat identified annoyance in his expression. They might have shared a second of physical awareness, they might have daughters the same age and in the same class, but they were still very much adversaries.

'No problem,' Kat said, meeting his gaze with defiance and giving free rein to the immaturity she might have been able to fight if she hadn't had such a strong physical reaction to the hateful man. 'We were happy to be *flexible* as you were clearly held up.'

She threw his words from that morning back at him, her smile falsely sweet.

So she played by the book—there were times when her planning and checklists and reliability came in very handy, like it had today.

Reading her dig loud and clear, Nash narrowed his eyes. 'I wasn't held up.' He'd lowered his voice in a way that told Kat he didn't want Molly to overhear, but she was once more giggling with Lucy, oblivious to the tension between the adults.

'I called the school, informed them there'd been a last-minute change of Molly's mother's plans. I don't owe you any explanation, but if

I'd been scheduled to pick her up I'd have been here on time.'

As if reminded of her mother's absence once more, Molly glanced at the adults, her laughter fading. Kat backed down. Before Nash had arrived she'd been careful not to judge Molly's mother for being five minutes late. She didn't want the return of Molly's tears. Nor did she want the girls to witness a continuation of her previous standoff with Nash, not when their daughters were so obviously enamoured of one another.

'Well, you're here now and I'm actually glad. The girls had me trapped in the middle of a tricky negotiation involving the park where I was outnumbered.' She offered him a hesitant smile, hoping for the girls' sake they could put their spat behind them.

'Daddy, can Lucy come to the park with us?' Molly asked, her eyes pleading.

Nash looked as cornered as Kat felt.

'I think it's time we headed home, actually,' she said. The last thing she wanted was to spend any more time with him than was absolutely necessary given her body's absurd physical attraction to him.

'It looks like Lucy's mum is too busy for the park,' Nash said, smiling down at his daughter before flicking a triumphant look Kat's way.

Seeing the challenge for what it was, Kat held his stare. No way would she play the bad cop to his good cop. He'd already made her appear uptight and rigid once today because they had different ways of doing things. But Kat could be fun and spontaneous. If he thought throwing down the gauntlet would scare her off, he was wrong. She could tolerate his insufferable company for ten more minutes for the sake of their daughters.

'Actually, we'd love to see the park, wouldn't we, Luce?' Kat said, her chin raised in defiance.

It wasn't until she was forced to walk beside him in awkward silence while the girls ran ahead that she fully appreciated the enormity of her error.

Their ridiculous game of one-upmanship meant there was no escaping him or the way he made her feel both antagonistic and helplessly aroused.

CHAPTER FOUR

GRADY WALKED AT Kat's side behind their girls, willing away the last of his annoyance with Carol for being so utterly unreliable. The minute he'd arrived at school to see the distress and uncertainty on his daughter's face, he'd had only one goal: getting to her as soon as possible, engulfing her in a soothing hug and hoping that it would be enough to take away her pain and confusion.

Why had he given Carol the opportunity to let Molly down once more, today of all days? He should have known from past experience that her selfishness wouldn't make her think twice about picking up an extra shift at work at the last minute and leaving him scrambling to make it to the school on time. She pulled stunts like this all the time.

He should never have capitulated to Carol in the first place. If he'd stuck to the arrangements that had been in place for months he'd have been at school before the bell rang.

Aware of the light floral scent of Kat at his side, close enough that the hairs on his arms stood to attention, Grady silently cursed his luck that Kat had been there to witness the upset Carol had caused. She already had a pretty low opinion of him. But worse, because of his own pig-headedness and the way he'd allowed her to rattle him, he now had to spend even more time in her company.

Seeing Molly laugh with her friend after the inevitable tears of earlier was all the reward he needed for his self-inflicted torture. He'd give Molly the moon if he could. Being stuck with the most infuriating woman he'd ever been attracted to was a small price to pay for his daughter's smile.

'You know—' Kat spoke over the excited chatter coming from their daughters '—if you or Molly's mum are ever stuck at work or running late, Lucy and I would be happy to wait with Molly until you get here. They obviously get on like two peas in a pod.'

He glanced her way, caught the indulgent smile on her face as she watched their daughters giggle together, Lucy's blonde head next to Molly's brown. Was she having another dig at him because he'd been five minutes late to collect Molly?

He shouldn't care what she thought of him. When it came to parenting his daughter, Grady was his own severest critic. The only person he cared about being answerable to was Molly. That was why he kept on giving Carol the benefit of the doubt, always hoping that she'd step up and be the mother that Molly deserved. He never wanted his daughter to one day blame him that she and Carol had no relationship.

Sometimes, just like during his marriage, he couldn't win no matter what he did.

'Is that your idea of an apology?' he asked, trying to forget the way she'd felt pressed up against his chest for the split second they'd collided. He could still feel the soft mounds of her breasts, still see the way her pupils had dilated when their eyes had met, still hear the sexy little sound of her shocked gasp.

No wonder he was being paranoid. His brain was poisoned by testosterone.

'No,' she said. 'I just thought, as you're probably as relaxed about time-keeping as you are for the rules, that I'd offer.'

Acknowledging that some of his testiness was aimed at Carol not Kat, he scrubbed a hand over his face, biting back a retort.

'As I said,' he replied, because a part of him, the part he'd assumed was as good as done with women, couldn't have Kat thinking that he was blasé when it came to parenting, 'I wasn't late or held up. Molly's mother was supposed to pick her up, but couldn't at the last minute.'

Despite them having a shared custody arrangement, Carol's job as a flight attendant, and the way she seemed to find parenting mundane, meant that Molly lived practically full-time with Grady. For himself, he couldn't be happier with the arrangement, but even while keen to foster Molly's relationship with Carol, he wished it could be different for Molly's sake. But he should have known that Carol being a part Molly's first day at school would end in tears. Twice.

'Of course,' Kat said, surprising him with her understanding, although it was probably aimed at Carol, not him. 'Things come up.'

Uninterested in Kat's opinion of his fathering skills, he walked in silence for a few minutes. He might tolerate her criticisms at work, but since the moment he'd heard about Carol's pregnancy he'd moved mountains to be the best father he could be.

He didn't want the mistakes he and Carol had made to affect their little girl, even though at times, like today, he was doomed to fail one way or another.

'Is your…um…wife in medicine too?' Kat asked when they reached the playground.

'Ex-wife,' he said with emphasis. He and Carol had been long over even before the divorce. 'No, she isn't. She's a flight attendant.'

'Oh… I see.' Kat fell quiet.

'Let me guess,' he said. 'You don't approve of divorce.' The part of him struggling with the chemistry he felt every time they were together, whether she was confronting him or not, couldn't resist the opportunity to point out their differences.

'Why would you say that?' she asked, shocked.

He shrugged, keeping his eyes on the girls as they ran ahead towards the swings. 'Because you're a stickler for the rules type of person.'

Not for the first time, he wondered what her story was. She didn't wear a wedding ring, but a husband, fiancé or even a boyfriend would be really convenient in helping him to forget his attraction and see her as nothing more than a work colleague.

When he turned to face her, she was gaping. It made him aware of her soft-looking lips and the pink of her tongue.

Kat fisted her hands on her hips. 'For your

information, I've never been married. It's just me and Lucy.'

Grady's pulse kicked up. 'So, Lucy's father isn't part of the picture?'

His body's enthusiastic response to the news that she was single made no difference. Just because he found her attractive didn't mean he intended to act on it. Beyond their marital status and their daughters, and their jobs, they had zero in common.

'No.' Kat shook her head and looked away, but not before he'd seen the flash of vulnerability in her eyes. 'He lives in the UK.' She immediately frowned as if regretting her candour.

Gobsmacked, Grady allowed his curiosity for the woman he'd vowed to avoid to bloom. Was this ex the reason she was so prickly, so defensive? Had he hurt her? He wanted to ask who'd left who. Kat certainly didn't seem the type to deliberately flout convention.

Then he checked himself. He wasn't interested in the answers. He was only tolerating her company because she made him uncharacteristically confrontational.

Except that flash of pain in her eyes, the way her chin had tilted when she'd said *It's just me and Lucy...*' It called to the nurse in him.

'Being a single parent is hard,' he said, empathetic towards her in a way he'd have sworn was impossible half an hour ago. 'Especially when you work full-time in a stressful field, the way we do.'

She eyed him grudgingly, her wary expression back. Then she conceded with a small nod.

For a few minutes they watched in silence as the girls took turns on a blue plastic slide. Despite her story, despite them being complete opposites personality-wise, Kat was clearly a good mother. Lucy seemed delightful. Her job was demanding, and he knew from Lauren that she was also studying for her professional emergency medicine exams.

If only Carol was as constant in Molly's life.

Before he could once more ruminate how his marital failure continued to have consequences for his little girl, Kat spoke.

'Look, about this morning—I feel like I owe you an apology.'

Grady couldn't believe his ears. He forced himself to meet her stare, to ignore the uncertainty he saw there. It would be easier to dismiss his attraction if she stayed neatly inside the box he'd assigned her to after their difference of opinion: not a team player. But they still had to find a way to work together.

Seeing his doubtful expression, she ploughed on. 'I was intent on making a good impression on my first day. I hate mistakes, but I'm not too uptight to admit that I probably overcompensated.'

Probably?

'Okay,' he said, stalling for time. The last thing he wanted was to complicate his life with another tricky relationship, even if it was only at work. Carol provided all the turmoil and disruption he would ever need.

But Kat wasn't done with her speech.

'It's obvious that Lucy and Molly get along.' She smiled over to where their daughters were contemplating the monkey bars.

A twinge of regret lodged under his ribs. His frustration with his ex meant that he too had played his part in the battleground of Kat's first day at Gulf Harbour. That wasn't him.

'I'm happy to put our difference of opinion behind us for the sake of their friendship,' she said, then nibbled at her lush lower lip in a totally distracting way. 'What do you say?' She held out her hand for him to shake, her smile stretching into the open version he'd found so attractive when they were first introduced that morning.

Then, like now, it left Grady disconcerted. He didn't want to find her appealing. He enjoyed his job, the only area of his life Carol couldn't upset, unlike Kat. The potential for misunderstandings and differences of opinion should steer him back to his original plan to manipulate the staff rota so they saw as little of each other as possible.

But there was something about Kat Collins, beyond the chemistry, that made him want to grasp the proffered olive branch. Who knew, perhaps they'd end up friends. Lauren, Grady's oldest friend at the hospital, had certainly sung Kat's praises today.

'Sure.' He took her hand in a brief shake that wasn't brief enough, because it sparked his keen awareness of her once more: the softness of her skin, the quirky, lopsided slant to her smile, the allure of her intelligence and strength of character.

'Great. That's sorted,' she said, laughter in her eyes as she headed over to the swings, pushing Lucy and then Molly higher and higher until they squealed.

As he watched her uninhibited delight transform her face from beautiful to breathtaking, he realised that he'd have his work cut out for him managing his attraction to Gulf Harbour's newest doctor. Just because their daughters were going to be friends didn't mean Grady needed to personally ensnare himself with another woman who was on a different wavelength and found him lacking.

All he had to do was wait for his body to get the message.

Easy.

CHAPTER FIVE

TWO DAYS LATER, in response to an urgent call, Kat pushed through the doors of the resuscitation room. One of the ER house officers was alone with an elderly patient who was clearly having a grand mal seizure, his arms and legs jerking violently.

No sooner had Kat joined the overwhelmed-looking young doctor at the head of the unresponsive patient than Nash arrived.

Quickly assessing the situation, Kat and Nash manoeuvred the patient onto his side to protect his airway. Kat reached for a nearby nasopharyngeal tube and oxygen mask. Nash connected the patient to the monitors that recorded his vital signs, each of them anticipating the other's moves as they worked quickly with practised moves to stabilise the patient.

'What is the history?' Kat asked the house officer. The woman recited the brief clinical presentation that she'd managed to glean, while

Nash drew some blood for the lab. The man, who had no known history of epilepsy, had presented in the ER with confusion and other non-specific symptoms of headache and fatigue. The house officer had been about to examine him when he collapsed and the seizure began.

'Can you please get me four milligrams of Lorazepam?' she asked Nash, who nodded and retrieved the drugs from the locked cupboard on the wall.

Returning to the bedside, Nash grunted with frustration. 'The cannula has tissued,' he said to Kat, reaching for a new one.

'We can use intramuscular midazolam instead,' Kat said, although they both knew that IV was better.

Nash shook his head and applied a tourniquet around the patient's other arm. 'If I can't gain venous access on the first try, we'll switch to midazolam.'

Kat bit her tongue, torn because IV would enter the bloodstream quicker, but in the time it might take Nash to insert another cannula they could have already administered the intramuscular injection.

He quickly set about inserting a new cannula into the other arm, expertly achieving it on the first go; no mean feat considering the continuing seizure.

But Kat had no time to be impressed.

With the IV treatment administered, Nash took over airway maintenance while Kat examined the patient for signs of head trauma and then scanned the notes for any clue that might explain the patient's seizure.

'That's four minutes with no change,' Nash said, his gaze meeting Kat's loaded with meaning.

Kat nodded. 'Thanks for keeping count.' The longer the patient remained unconscious the greater the chance of serious complications like brain damage.

Staving off the instinctive panic the adrenaline coursing through her blood was causing, Kat took a few seconds to mentally work through the emergency protocol for status epilepticus, a prolonged, life-threatening seizure. She felt Nash looking to her for a decision, aware that he most likely would have his own way of handling the emergency, but a niggle in the back of her mind made her stick to her protocol.

'Have you checked a blood glucose?' she asked the junior doctor as she administered the second dose of intravenous drugs in an attempt to stop the seizure.

'Um…not yet, no.'

'That's five minutes, Kat. Do you want to intubate?' Nash reached for an endotracheal tube and glanced her way expectantly.

Newly aware of their fragile truce and their disagreement on her first day, Kat hesitated. He'd called her a stickler for the rules. She didn't see that as a flaw. She'd once lost control of her life, a situation that had caused a lot of pain to a lot of people, not just her. Rules and routines gave her control back, along with a modicum of peace. She should trust her instincts.

Injecting her voice with certainty, she answered Nash. 'No. Keep bagging him; his sats are good.'

Kat ignored Nash's small frown, which told her he'd have done things differently, and spoke to the other doctor. 'Do the glucose now, please. We need to know if there's something treatable causing this fit.'

'Don't you want to consider a second line treatment?' Nash said, casting Kat a look that told her he disagreed with her management of the case. Yes, they needed to treat the seizure, but if there was an underlying and easily treatable cause it needed to be excluded.

'Protocol is to concurrently exclude a reversible cause,' she said, sticking to the flowchart she knew by heart, even though his confidence and gut instinct to try for venous access had been the right one.

But, just like she hadn't questioned him pushing for the second IV, he didn't question her insisting on the blood test.

Within seconds of performing the finger prick test for blood glucose, the sheepish-looking house officer returned. 'Blood sugar is less than two. I'm sorry.'

'You were right—hypoglycaemia,' Nash said as he attached an intravenous glucose infusion to the cannula he'd inserted and gave Kat a nod of respect.

Tense seconds followed while they watched and waited.

Kat was about to ask for the second line anticonvulsive drugs when the seizure stopped.

All three of them breathed a collective sigh of relief.

'Always check blood glucose,' Kat instructed the house officer. 'And check all of his blood work—electrolytes, toxicology, blood gases. Also, see if you can get a better history from a relative or his GP. Is he on any medications that might be causing hypoglycaemia, or does he have a history of alcohol abuse?'

The doctor nodded, spurred into action now that the emergency had eased.

Kat spoke to the medical registrar, who had just arrived, handing over the patient's care.

She drew aside the curtains, preparing to

leave, to return to the patient she'd been seeing prior to the emergency call. Some inexplicable drive made her look back at Nash.

Their eyes met, silent communication passing between them. They were different in every way. They would likely always have different methods, approach the same situation from different angles, but at the end of the day they'd just proved that when required they could work as a team.

'Thanks,' she said.

'Good call,' he replied.

Kat left, buoyed up not only by a sense of job satisfaction that she'd managed to help the patient, but worryingly also by Nash's unexpected praise.

Later that week, Kat emerged from the ED's minor injuries clinic to find Nash talking with Lauren. Loitering near one of the workstations, Kat surreptitiously watched them chatting, her attention drawn to Nash as if he were a specimen under a microscope. The friends laughed about something, and a prickle of absurd jealousy made Kat's temperature rise.

Nash's broad, relaxed smile mesmerised her; she couldn't look away. Just like she'd been fascinated when he'd unselfconsciously goofed around in the playground with both girls on their first day. Or when his smile crinkled the corners of his eyes when he laughed with a patient. And most distracting of all was how well he wore hospital scrubs, as if the baggy functional garments that made everyone else look sickly were specifically created with his physique and colouring in mind.

The easygoing version of Nash laughing with Lauren seemed to be the one that everyone else saw. Since her first day, Kat had quickly discovered that the man capable of pressing her buttons more effectively than anyone else had a reputation throughout the hospital as a straight up nice guy. He was universally adored by the patients. Nothing about the day-to-day running of the department was too much trouble for him, but neither was he a pushover. He just got things done, quietly and efficiently, always patient-focused.

Flushed from how much more attractive his reliability made him, and frustrated by the persistence of her silly hormonal urges, Kat dragged her gaze away from the pair.

Despite their truce and the way they'd compromised on the management of the seizure patient, there was still a brick wall of wariness between him and Kat. She sighed, wishing the tension would just evaporate because Lucy and

Molly's friendship was going from strength to strength.

Keeping her head down, she tried to slink past Nash and Lauren unnoticed.

Just as Kat was almost home free and around the corner out of sight, Lauren called her name. 'Kat!'

Kat froze, plastered a breezy smile on her face and joined her boss and Nash.

'How are you settling in?' Lauren asked, her sharply intelligent eyes searching Kat's stare as if the woman were a human lie detector. Would Lauren sense the awkwardness between her and Nash? Had he spoken to the departmental head about their clashes?

'Um…good, I think.' Kat shot Nash a sideways glance, her heart thudding excitedly behind her sternum.

Why couldn't she just dismiss his charm, exaggerate his negatives, switch off her body's animal responses? It would make life so much easier if she wasn't attracted to him.

Because Nash and Lauren were both still looking at her expectantly, as if she'd walked into the middle of a conversation where she was the main topic, Kat added, 'Everyone has been extremely welcoming and helpful, and I seem to have a handle on how things work here now.'

Now that she'd settled in, Gulf Harbour ER seemed like a great department in which to work.

'Well,' Lauren said, shooting Nash a pointed stare, 'as Grady here seems to have temporarily forgotten his manners, *I'll* do the honours. Come and join us at The Har-Bar tomorrow night.'

Kat opened her mouth to mumble some excuse, but was cut off.

'It's Grady's birthday,' the other woman added. 'I've just this minute persuaded him that it's something worth celebrating, so you're officially invited. You're not rostered on this weekend, are you?'

Kat tried not to squirm in discomfort, her cheeks warming as her back hit the proverbial wall. She couldn't refuse her boss. Nor could she decline without it appearing like she was still harbouring a grudge against Nash.

'Um…no…no, I'm not.' Kat looked anywhere other than at Nash. She didn't want to witness his irritation or resignation now that he'd had his hand forced to invite her along.

This was awkward enough. It was obvious that Nash hadn't planned on inviting Kat himself. And why would he? They had nothing in common and she'd been avoiding him as much as she could since her first day, hoping to minimise further differences of opinion and still embarrassed by her physical crush.

Perhaps six years and counting of celibacy wasn't such a bright idea after all.

'Great, that's settled,' Lauren said with a self-satisfied smile. 'See you tomorrow.' Leaving Kat alone with Nash, Lauren strode away.

Now she'd have the added embarrassment of extricating herself from the invitation without letting him think she was offended that he hadn't wanted her along. The last thing she needed to be was the unwelcome guest at his birthday bash. Clearly, despite what they'd agreed in the park, they weren't going to be friends.

'Look—'

'Are you free now?' Nash interrupted and then apologised. 'I could do with a second opinion on a patient.'

Kat breathed a sigh of relief, grateful for the distraction of work.

'Of course, lead the way.' She followed him over to the workstation, where he logged in to the computer and brought up a patient's record.

'What's the case?' Kat asked, stepping close enough to see the screen while trying to ignore the heat of his body and the subtle scent of his aftershave that she remembered all too well from their playground collision.

'There's an eight-year-old in bay six,' he said, glancing her way so their eyes met.

Kat swallowed, praying her attraction wasn't transparent.

'He presented with general malaise, fever and coryzal symptoms, but I think he might have Koplik spots inside his mouth. I've only seen them in textbooks, so I wanted another pair of eyes.'

Why had he asked her and not Lauren for a second opinion?

'Any rash?' Kat asked, because Koplik spots were associated with measles, but could often appear first.

'No, not yet, but of relevance is that the child hasn't been vaccinated.' He turned to face her, crossed his arms over his chest, looked down, waiting.

A fresh wave of lust body-slammed her. She could still feel that strong arm preventing her from taking a tumble outside the classroom. For a second, before he'd focused all of his attention on his daughter, Kat had imagined her attraction was reciprocated. But she must have invented his interest.

'Okay,' Kat said, reaching for a face mask. 'Let's take a look.'

They entered the bay together. Kat introduced herself to the boy and his mother and performed a quick examination to exclude other common childhood infections that might be responsible for his symptoms. When she shone a torch into the boy's mouth, she instantly saw what had Nash concerned—small white spots lining the cheeks.

'I think you're right, Nash,' she said when they were once more out of earshot. 'Good spotting, excuse the pun.'

She laughed nervously. How could he make her feel giddy? Perhaps avoiding him wasn't the best plan. Perhaps she needed to flood her system with contact until she became immune.

'I've only seen Koplik spots a few times.' She removed her mask and tossed it into the bin, then washed her hands in the sink beside the one he was using. 'We can run measles serology and if it's positive we have to notify Public Health. Are you happy to tell the parents the diagnosis?'

Nash nodded, switching off the water at the other sink and drying his own hands with a paper towel. 'Thanks, Kat.'

For a second she froze, her stare locked to his, trapped. She should say something—anything—to break the tension. By doing her best to avoid him she'd only fuelled the flames of her attraction.

'Listen, don't feel like you have to come to

The Har-Bar tomorrow,' he said, as if sensing her discomfort, 'just because Lauren invited you.'

Kat busied herself with the paper towel dispenser on the wall while she willed her expression to stay neutral and not give away any hint of her inner deflation.

'Of course not,' she said, flashing him an overly bright smile that hopefully concealed the sting of rejection.

He was giving her a gentle escape route because he didn't want her there. It was the reminder she needed that her infatuation was one-sided.

'Kat…' Rather than move away and resume his duties, Nash stepped closer. The scent of clean laundry and spicy aftershave made her head a little woozy as her pulse throbbed in her throat.

She looked up, the pressure of meeting his searching stare making her eyes water.

A flashback of the way he'd doted on Molly and included Lucy in a game of tag sent another sharp pang of longing through her ribs. What would it feel like to be held in those strong arms? To be the focus of his desire? To feel those distracting lips brush hers?

Her throat was so dry she dared not speak.

'Just to be clear,' Nash said, dragging Kat's

mind away from her wildly inappropriate and probably one-sided thoughts. 'If Lauren had given me the chance, I'd planned on issuing a department-wide invitation for tomorrow night, which, of course, includes you.'

His gaze dipped from her eyes to her mouth.

For an exhilarating second Kat thought he might kiss her. Insane. They were at work and he'd shown no sign that he harboured the same attraction.

'But it's late notice.' His lips moved, killing Kat's wild flight of fancy. 'You'd need to find a babysitter. So don't stress if you can't make it.'

Babysitter…?

She shook her head, so distracted by the chemistry she just couldn't shake off that she'd almost forgotten about Lucy.

Lucy. Her child. Her responsibility.

No matter how much her body wanted to explore a flirtation with the first man she'd fancied in so long, Lucy would always come first.

'Yes, of course you're right.' Kat's voice was an embarrassing croak.

As if he'd overstepped some imaginary line, Nash moved back and her stomach dropped with disappointment.

'I would need to find a sitter,' she said, now horribly conflicted.

Whether Nash was interested in her was irrelevant. The often lonely and seriously neglected woman in her deserved a night out, a harmless drink with work colleagues. Her parents would probably be overjoyed to have Lucy for the night if it meant Kat being social; she just tried not to ask them for childcare favours too often as they'd already done so much for Kat after she'd returned from the UK.

Backing away, she cleared her throat. 'Well, thanks for the invite—I'll try and be there if I can.'

Hating his relaxed shrug, she turned away.

Henry's cold and cruel dismissal had robbed Kat of a vital chunk of self-esteem. Now, that damaged part of her wanted Nash to be disappointed if she couldn't make it.

She sighed. She was tying herself up like a bow with all her doubts and justifications, over-thinking a simple invitation. But, no matter how harmless the social event seemed, the past five minutes in his company had shown her one thing. When it came to Nash Grady, Kat's thoughts were still far from innocent. And that was proving to be a big problem.

CHAPTER SIX

GRADY TURNED FROM the bar, where he'd just bought Lauren a glass of wine, and almost spilled it down the front of his shirt. Kat had made it at last, just when he'd given up hope that she'd appear.

After all, she'd looked horrified by Lauren's invitation yesterday. When he'd tried to repair some of the damage by insisting that he'd always intended on including her in the invitation, she couldn't seem to run away quick enough, just like she'd been avoiding him all week, her head ducking when she assumed he hadn't spotted her around the department.

So much for friends…

Heading back to Lauren, who was having some relationship drama of her own tonight with her ex, Gulf Harbour's newest locum surgeon, Mason Ward, Grady stole another glance Kat's way.

She looked spectacular in her civvie clothes—

skinny black jeans, heels and a silky top that exposed one tanned and freckled shoulder—her hair loose in a wavy cascade and her eyes bright and animated as she laughed with a group of the ER staff.

He couldn't seem to stop staring.

While he chatted with Lauren, who was constantly watching the door for Mason, Grady tried to ignore the rumble of arousal Kat's arrival caused. He wanted to speak to her, to thank her for coming along to celebrate his birthday when he knew that meant she'd organised childcare. He knew how hard it was to juggle everything.

Every time he moved in her direction he kept being drawn into other conversations—people wishing him Happy Birthday, enquiring after Molly or making a joke about his advanced age.

When he finally made it to Kat's group and thanked everyone for coming, she was too far away, opposite him in the small huddle of people, her stare only meeting his for a fraction of a second.

He went through the motions of contributing to the conversation while restless energy coiled inside him. All he really wanted to do was speak to Kat one-on-one. Every time he looked at her, she blinked, smiled, looked away. It was driving him nuts. One minute he was certain that she was as into him as he was to her and the next convinced it was all in his head.

He felt sixteen again, in the throes of a desperate crush but clueless as to the recipient's feelings.

Clearly, no matter what he tried, it wasn't going to be easy to get his attraction to Kat out of his system. And it was no wonder. Not only was she sexy and smart and a great mother but, despite their differences, despite their first day disagreement, they also somehow just clicked professionally. His respect for her had gone through the roof as they'd collaborated on the seizure patient. The dauntless look in her eyes and the determined tilt of her chin had told him that she'd disagreed with his suggestions on more than one occasion. But they'd made it through together, worked out their differences when it counted to treat the patient.

Kat excused herself from the group and headed for the bathrooms. Grady chatted to a few more people while he waited for her to return. Noticing that Lauren and Mason had disappeared, Grady texted his friend, concerned.

Somewhere between bidding farewell to a handful of guests and watching the door for Lauren's return, he realised that Kat seemed to have disappeared.

The taste of disappointment soured what

should have been an enjoyable evening so that ten minutes later, with most of the guests departed, Grady too left The Har-Bar, frustrated that Kat had left without saying goodbye.

He kicked a stray pebble along the pavement and headed for the car park behind the bar. It was a lost cause. Clearly she wanted nothing to do with him outside of work and that suited him just fine. His life was complicated enough. He'd barely made it to his own birthday drinks, because Carol had tried to talk to him about them getting back together when he'd dropped Molly off at her place. It was a stunt she tried every six months or so, even though he always gave her the same answer: a resounding no.

At his car and before he could open the door, his thoughts were interrupted by the unmistakable sound of an engine turning over, an exercise in futility. Someone was having trouble starting their car.

Weary but unable to ignore a person in need, he approached the vehicle and tapped on the passenger window, his heart lurching when Kat looked up.

Her shock turned to relief as she recognised him in the dark.

'Are you okay?' Grady smiled, glad now that he hadn't minded his own business and thanking his lucky stars. Not that he wished a breakdown on her. But this was the chance he'd craved all evening—him and Kat alone. No children, no patients, no colleagues.

She opened the car door. 'Hi—it won't start for some reason.' She gave the ignition another go, as if to prove the point.

They both winced at the dull clicking sound.

'I don't understand why,' she said. 'The battery is only six months old, and I definitely didn't leave the lights on.'

She exited the car with a deep sigh of frustration, looking to him for a suggestion.

'I could offer to look under the bonnet, but with modern cars it's most likely something electrical that I won't have a clue how to fix.'

'No, don't worry. Thanks anyway.' She reached inside for her bag and took out her phone, closing the car door with more force than needed.

Perhaps she didn't want his help.

'Do you have roadside assistance?' he said anyway.

Kat was an intelligent, independent woman who could organise her own rescue, but he didn't like the idea of her waiting alone in that car park, not with the bars emptying soon. He indicated his own car, parked several spaces away. 'You can wait in my car if you want.'

'I do, but I don't fancy waiting around for

them now. I'll call them in the morning, ask my mum to give me a lift back here.'

Grady nodded. 'Do you want a lift home? I've been on soft drinks all night.' Even though he was the birthday boy and Molly was spending a rare night at Carol's house, he'd begun the habit after Molly's diagnosis of asthma, because he just never knew when he might need to drive her to the hospital in an emergency. 'You probably need to get back to relieve your sitter,' he added, conscious of holding her up.

And driving her home would give them a chance to talk.

'Um…' She blinked up at him, looking a little flustered while she debated her response. 'I don't have to worry about that—Lucy is staying the night with my parents.' She glanced at her phone, chewing on her lip. 'I'd call them now, but they've probably already gone to bed. Lucy tends to wear them out when she stays over.'

'Thanks though,' she said, her voice ever so slightly breathless. 'I appreciate the offer.' She smiled that crooked smile of hers and the current of awareness, the connection he might have imagined pulsed anew.

Grady hesitated. He couldn't leave until he knew she was safe, but he wouldn't force his offer of a lift onto her either.

'Okay…' He stepped back a pace. 'Well… I

just wanted to thank you for coming tonight. I know it's not easy when you have to organise childcare. I really appreciate it.'

Saying what he'd hoped to say gave him no sense of satisfaction. Probably because close up she looked even prettier than she had from afar.

'You're welcome,' she said, staring up at him with uncertainty. Then she started, as if remembering something, touched his arm. 'Oh, wait.'

Grady's nervous system ignited like a lit box of fireworks after that single touch of her hand. Her perfume tickled his nose, reminding him of the sunset from his deck on a sultry summer night, the scent of jasmine carried on the warm air.

Looking embarrassed, she pulled a slightly battered card from the back pocket of her jeans and thrust it his way. 'Happy Birthday.'

'Thanks.' He couldn't help his grin as he tore into the envelope, which was still warm from her body heat. The spark of excitement in her eyes felt like the best birthday gift he'd ever received.

The card depicted a cartoon girl flying through the air on a swing, the caption *Life's Short, Swing High* underneath. Inside it was simply signed *from Kat and Lucy*.

It reminded him of their trip to the park when he'd seen Kat's fun side as she'd taken a turn on the swings alongside Lucy and Molly, making who could go the highest into a game. He'd been forced to take a second look at Kat and adjust his first impressions.

Except that had only left him hungry for more information.

'I completely forget to give it to you earlier. Sorry that it's a bit bent,' Kat said with a shrug, as if justifying her gesture.

'Thank you, Kat,' he said, strangely touched. 'It's a great sentiment.' He forced his stare away from her lush lips, from her satisfied little smile.

Their eyes locked.

Grady's pulse kicked up, his body urging him to test his theory that Kat Collins shared the sexual chemistry he could no longer deny. But something held him back, some hangover of his bad marriage. He no longer rushed into things, not since his divorce. And even if he was right that she shared his attraction, that didn't mean he should act on it, nor that Kat would want to.

'Look,' he said, tucking the card and envelope into his shirt pocket, 'I'm not going to be able to leave until I know you're safe, so you can wait in my car for your ride, or you can accept my lift home. It's really no big deal, in fact you'd be doing me a favour. I don't want to worry until our next shift together that you fell victim to some kind of foul play.'

'Foul play?' She laughed, her head tipping up, exposing her neck.

He nodded, totally distracted by her soft-looking skin, wondering if it would feel as good against his lips, if she'd smell as fantastic close up as she did from a polite distance.

'It's true what everyone says about you, isn't it?' With her eyes still dancing with humour, her gaze traced his face, assessing him on what felt like a whole new level. 'You're just a really nice guy.'

Grady shrugged, his head full of the more than nice things he'd like to do with her. 'I can be sometimes.'

She pressed her lips together as if she too might be thinking dirty thoughts. Then she came to a decision 'Okay. I'd love a lift. Thanks, Nash.'

Grady swallowed hard as he headed for his car. She was sticking to the first name thing and from the way *Nash* sounded on her lips he couldn't say he minded one little bit. Unlocking his car, he opened the passenger side door for Kat before rounding the bonnet and climbing into the driver's seat.

'So, where is Molly tonight?' Kat asked as

she clicked her seatbelt into place and looked over at him.

The interior of the car was dark, her face illuminated by the streetlight outside. She was inspecting him in a way that left him hot under the collar.

He cleared his tight throat. 'She's at her mum's place tonight, although she often stays with my parents at weekends, especially if I have to cover a night shift.'

He left the car park, pulled onto the road and headed for Kat's suburb.

'Do your parents help out with Lucy a lot?' he asked, because he had first-hand experience of the childcare struggles faced by most single working parents.

Kat nodded. 'I'm so lucky to have them, otherwise my job would be a lot harder. So, do you and your ex share custody?'

'Carol,' he clarified with a shrug. 'Kind of.'

The last thing he wanted to discuss with this woman who had driven him to distraction all night, while her birthday card was burning a hole through his shirt, was the mess of his post-divorce *relationship* with his ex-wife, which largely consisted of disagreements over Molly, or Carol just doing whatever the hell she pleased and then trying to persuade him that they should be a proper family again.

Kat frowned at his cryptic response. 'Oh… That sounds…complicated.'

'Yeah,' Grady admitted, a stab of familiar guilt jabbing between his ribs at his betrayal of the woman he'd once loved enough to make Molly with, to marry, to quit the army and put their family first with. The ashamed part of him, the part that had rushed into that relationship, the part that felt he hadn't truly known Carol until things had started to go wrong, wanted to hide from Kat and what was an easy, light flirtation.

'We do have a shared custody agreement,' he said, trying to keep the pointless bitterness from his voice, 'but I'm essentially Molly's parent full-time. Carol travels a lot with her job.'

That was generous of him. Carol's career in the airline industry was another choice she'd made after the divorce, almost as if she needed an excuse to abandon the parts of parenthood she found monotonous.

'That must be hard on you and Molly,' Kat said. 'That's what happened on the first day of school, right? She had to work?'

Grady felt her inquisitive stare burn the side of his face as he kept his eyes on the road. He fought the urge to over-share. He didn't want to badmouth Carol but, for some inexplicable reason, he also didn't feel comfortable lying to Kat.

'Yes, she did. I just wish she'd given me a little more warning so I could have managed Molly's disappointment. Do you mind if we change the subject?' He glanced her way, catching her wince of embarrassment.

'Of course. Sorry. I'm being nosy.'

'It's okay. I'm curious about your situation too, for the record. I'm just…conscious that she'll always be Molly's mother, and for Molly's sake I want them to have a good relationship.' Although he had his work cut out for him with Carol's erratic and unreliable attitude to parenting.

He stopped at the lights and glanced at Kat.

Her bottom lip trapped under her teeth, she was looking him over as if he were a fascinating new species she'd discovered. 'I have to say I'm impressed. I can spout an unending stream of vitriol regarding Lucy's father.' She laughed, but then clarified. 'Never in front of her, of course.'

'He really hurt you, huh?' Grady said, his eyes on the road once more. His instincts had been right; Kat had been badly let down by this British guy.

'You could say that,' she admitted flatly. 'But at least I get Lucy all to myself. One of the perks of making a baby with the wrong man.'

Grady nodded, unable to imagine the precise, rule-abiding Kat ever making something as human as a mistake. Nash's money was on her ex, who'd obviously monumentally messed up.

'Does Lucy ever see her father?' he asked. Although he sometimes despaired at Carol's broken promises, cursed her for letting their daughter down, Molly's first day of school being a prime example, Molly at least had some contact with her mother.

But perhaps a total absence would hurt Molly less.

'No, he doesn't, and before you suggest that I deliberately moved home to New Zealand to make it hard for him, you should know that the minute I told him I was pregnant he bailed on the two of us and never looked back.'

If he'd thought he'd heard her angry the day he'd admitted her patient to the orthopaedic ward, now she was all but spitting nails. No wonder. Kat was a smart, driven woman. It would really sting to be discarded, to have Lucy treated that way too.

'Just for the record, I'd never suggest you capable of such a thing,' he said, his voice tight with genuine regret for her situation. 'I'm sorry to hear that you and Lucy were so badly let down.'

Grady knew exactly how it felt to be disappointed by someone you'd once loved. How the rejection would be compounded tenfold if it also included your child.

'The guy sounds like an idiot,' he said, trying to lighten the atmosphere.

'I agree.' Kat laughed, her eyes dancing with flickers from the streetlights.

'What?' he asked at her continued enigmatic smile.

She shrugged. 'Who knew that a stickler for protocol and a rule-bender would agree on anything?'

'Not me.' He laughed, warmed inside to see her opening up, playful, flirtatious even. But along with their daughters and their work, they also had one more thing in common: their messy past relationships. No matter how much he wanted to kiss her and see if the chemistry was imagined or real, instinct told him to keep things friendly.

Trouble was, he couldn't deny that he was wildly attracted to Kat Collins.

With an internal sigh, he silently recited the words his wise five-year-old said when something went wrong: *Not good...not good at all.*

CHAPTER SEVEN

KAT HELD HER breath as the last rock-solid misconception she held of Nash crumbled to dust, unearthing more and more of his undeniably attractive facets.

She knew from the trip to the park that he was a great father, despite what sounded like a tricky situation with Molly's mother. He was even driving goodness knew how far out of his way to drop her home. And just like he was an outstanding and experienced nurse but demonstrated enough humility to ask for her help, like he had with the measles case, Kat could admit that thanks to Henry and the intuition and trust she could no longer rely upon, she'd grossly misjudged Nash's character.

Glancing over at her from the driver's seat, he smiled, the sexy crinkle around his eyes flipping her stomach. Her stare traced his strong profile and the subtle wave in his glossy dark hair. If only she could trust her libido and take what was becoming increasingly clear was a mutual attraction to the next level. Except the last person she'd slept with was Henry. The Kat who'd come back to New Zealand, alone and pregnant and forced to move back in with her parents, had vowed to be a better judge of the male character.

And then motherhood and work and being there for her parents after her father's stroke had consumed all of her time and energy. Now she was so rusty at flirtation it was a joke.

Wishing she'd scraped a razor over her legs in the shower earlier, just in case she found some unmined well of liberating bravery, Kat shelved her dithering for the time being.

'So,' she said, 'how long have you been divorced, and do you date much?'

Oh, real subtle. Perhaps she should ask him to switch on the car's air conditioning to cool herself down.

He took her probing questions in his stride, his deep laugh a comforting sound. 'I've been divorced for coming up to five years and dating isn't a priority for me at the moment, not when Molly is so little. How about you?'

Kat swallowed hard, nerves gripping her throat in a stranglehold. But she wasn't marrying him, only considering sleeping with him.

'I'm a single mother who works forty-eight

hours a week—what do you think?' She rolled her eyes, the sarcasm in her voice preferable to the self-pity she tried to keep at bay every time she considered her barren personal life. She was twenty-nine, not eighty-nine. Until she'd met Nash, she'd managed to convince herself that she no longer had any use for the opposite sex. But she owed it to herself to explore this chemistry. She wasn't imagining his interest, her body's reaction every time their eyes met telling her the attraction was mutual.

But was she ready to take the plunge after so long? She might as well be about to do a bungee jump for all the activity going on inside her abdomen.

Nash smiled, his gaze lingering a little too long. 'I know what you mean. Being a single parent is tough when it comes to dating.'

Kat nodded, relieved that she could share some of her feelings on the subject. Although sympathetic, none of her married friends understood. 'It's hard enough sneaking the time for a haircut or to take some exercise. Considering that side of your life just feels…somehow selfish.' Just as Henry had once accused her of being because she'd made the choice to have their baby.

'I know what you mean.' He nodded in agreement. 'As it is there just doesn't seem to be enough hours in the day.'

'And the last thing you need is to use up energy you don't have to develop or maintain any sort of relationship, even a casual one.' She pressed her lips together, scared she might have over-shared in her enthusiasm to talk to someone who understood. It was easier to ignore her sexual side, and until Nash she'd been doing a great job.

'I agree, most of the time,' he said, pensive.

Kat watched him pull into her street, curious now if he ever experienced loneliness, like her. Her heart rate accelerated so high she thought she might pass out.

'Most of the time?' she asked as, following her directions, he parked next to her driveway. Her weatherboard villa sat on a rear section, set back from the street behind another house.

He turned off the ignition and faced her, his expression hidden in shadow but his eyes mesmerising. 'I try to remember that we're human beings. We have biological needs that it's healthy to occasionally address.'

Kat nodded, not trusting her voice, her own biological needs clamouring to be heard after she'd shoved them aside for so long.

'My house is down that driveway,' she finally croaked when the pressure of meeting his gaze burned her eyes. It was decision time. Invite him in or say goodnight.

'I'll walk you to the door,' he said, exiting the car before she could protest.

The doubts rooted by Henry's rejection returned. It had been so long since she'd done this. No matter how much she wanted to be seen as a sophisticated professional woman who navigated her own destiny, inside she was a quivering mess.

Postponing the decision for a few more seconds, Kat walked at his side down the long, dark driveway, every step knotting her stomach a little tighter. It wasn't until they'd walked halfway down the drive that the motion sensor security light activated, flooding the property, and her and Nash, in its bright halogen beam.

He smiled, and her panic eased until the awkward moment on the doorstep. Kat hadn't trusted her instincts for over six years. But perhaps that was the biggest reason of all that she should stop over-thinking and just act on their chemistry.

Nash was a mature, responsible man with his own baggage. They had way more in common than she'd originally assumed. He was no more looking for a relationship than Kat. They could just have one night and then pretend it hadn't happened.

'Thanks for the lift,' she said, pushing her key into the lock while she tried to get her heart rate under control.

'You're welcome,' he said, looking up at her from the step below. 'Thanks again for joining us tonight. I'm glad you made it.'

Sick of her fear and hesitations, she leaned forward and brushed his cheek with her lips. 'Happy Birthday, Nash.'

She pulled back, her head swimming from lack of oxygen, her hand staying on his shoulder. Her lips tingled where his stubble had grazed them, his scent a disorienting cloud, filling her mind with the erotic possibilities she'd denied herself for so long. He smelled so good.

Instead of leaving, Nash regarded her intently, as if aware that her peck on the cheek was more than platonic.

Kat's overwrought brain made one last-ditch attempt to apply the brakes, her thoughts turning to the unopened box of condoms in her bathroom cabinet that had been there for years—a *time to get back in the saddle* joke gift from a friend. For all she knew, they had long since expired.

But she was done with denial. Henry had once decimated her self-esteem, made her feel unattractive and worthless. She deserved something for herself, didn't she?

Laying herself open, she curled her fingers into the fabric of his shirt, hoping he'd be left in no doubt of her desire.

As the feel of her lips on his cheek faded, her fingers gripping his shirt, Grady surrendered to the chemical attraction he'd been fighting since the first day he'd met Kat.

Before she changed her mind, he chased her lips with his, capturing her sensual mouth in a kiss that raised the stakes from the friendly peck on the cheek from which he might have walked away. But ignoring Kat's feminine sexuality was like ignoring a hurricane warning, something only a fool would do.

As his lips moved against hers, she shuddered, her body collapsing onto his chest as he held her close. Now that they'd surrendered to the first inevitable kiss, their mouths connected, as if magnetic.

Grady shut out all of the dismissals and justifications, the mental gymnastics he'd endured on the drive to Kat's place. It made no sense to fool around with a work colleague—his life was already complicated enough—but the minute she'd flexed her fingers against his shoulder, her vulnerable stare holding him captive, there was no reasoning with his desires.

Helpless to their connection, which as their

conversation in the car proved went beyond animal attraction, Grady allowed Kat to take everything she wanted from their kiss. Her fingers anchored in his hair, her breasts crushed up against his pecs and her soft moans urged him to part her lips and meet her tongue with his own, the surge and retreat a carnal exploration, each kiss more potent than the one before.

He'd known it would be this good from that collision in the playground, although he'd done his best to fight his instincts. Somewhere in his subconscious, the niggle of warning clamoured to be heard. She'd shared things with him tonight, intimate clues to her past and her struggles as a solo parent. He didn't want to lead her on, or complicate their working situation, but her lips tasted so good. She was making it so hard for him to think straight.

As if intent on torturing him further, Kat released a sexy little whimper against his lips, her hands sliding under the hem of his shirt to caress his back.

He growled, cupping her face, spearing his fingers into her hair and pushing her back against the door jamb so he could pin her there with his hips.

Any minute now he would put a stop to the kissing. Anything more required careful thought, a serious conversation, managed expectations in order to avoid misunderstanding or hurt feelings.

When Kat began to ride one of his thighs, which had somehow ended up between her legs, the last rational part of his brain shut down. He reciprocated, grinding his hardness into her stomach while he explored her mouth in slow but demanding swipes of his tongue that freed more of her sexy little moans.

Finally, maybe because he needed to breathe, he paused to gulp air. He looked down, lost for words at how quickly one kiss on the doorstep had escalated. Kat's lips were swollen, her stare pleasure drunk, her eyelids heavy.

She looked even more beautiful. He closed his eyes to block out the tempting sight.

'Don't stop,' she whispered, tugging his mouth back to hers.

His body hummed with desperation. He was done denying that he wanted her. But some kernel of doubt germinated. He needed to be sure that she wanted the same thing.

It almost killed him, but he pulled away once more. 'Kat…' Her lips followed his, her kisses swallowing the words he tried to speak. 'Are you sure this is a good idea?'

He wanted to do the right thing but she'd made him so worked up he was no longer sure what the right thing was.

She looked up at him, her expression dazed. 'Don't tell me you've decided to stop going with the flow. I thought I was the one who needed rules.'

At her continued tugging of his waist, Grady sighed and rested his forehead against hers. 'You are the one who needs rules. I just don't want there to be any misguided expectations.'

Kat's lips found his earlobe, the side of his neck. His eyes rolled back in his head as he fought for control over his libido.

'I want you, Nash, and I'm tired of fighting it. That doesn't mean I want more than sex, more than just one night. Consider those my rules if you want.'

Despite the fact that her lips and hands seemed to be everywhere at once, Grady forced himself to demand her attention. 'I want you too. But we work together and our situations are similar. I don't have any spare energy for a relationship.'

'Which is why you won't bend my rules: one night and then we pretend it didn't happen.' With a spark of challenge in her eyes, she turned the key in the lock and stepped over the threshold.

'It's like you said, Nash—we have biological needs.' She held out her hand, inviting him inside.

He took her hand in his, still hesitating on the other side of the front door. He cursed his own words from their conversation in the car. He'd been caught up in the moment, humbled that Kat felt comfortable enough with him to share some of her feelings. A part of him had wanted her to know that she deserved to consider her own needs, beyond her role as a doctor and a mother.

Wasn't that exactly what she was doing now?

He'd dallied for so long hesitation flickered across her face. 'I mean, I don't want to force you. I just thought—'

Before she could finish that sentence or doubt how much he wanted to follow her rules, he stepped into the hallway, closed the front door and hauled her into his arms for another kiss.

'Of course you're not forcing me,' he said when they parted for air. 'I'm only too happy to abide by your rules.'

Her smile dazzled him. 'Good. As long as you're not going to go off script and become all clingy on me.'

'I promise.' Because he felt ravenous without her mouth on his, he kissed her again, only pausing when she took his hand and guided him the few metres along the dark hallway to her bedroom.

Inside the room, Kat paused. They both glanced at the bed.

'I'm sorry,' she said, her teeth tugging at her bottom lip with sudden hesitation. 'I haven't done this for a while. Do you want a drink or something?'

Grady shook his head, tugging her into his arms and tilting her chin up so their stares locked. He traced the lip she'd chewed with his thumb. 'How long? I need to know if I should bring out my A game.' He smiled, trying to put her at ease.

Because he was still cupping her jaw, he felt her swallow. 'Six years,' she whispered.

Six years?

Grady tried not to gape at her shocking confession. That meant she hadn't slept with anyone since before Lucy was born, since the idiot who obviously broke her heart.

Her body tensed in his arms. Cupping her face, he gently caressed her lips with his, focused on how good her kisses felt, hoping that Kat would feel as good.

'In that case,' he said, sliding his hands under the hem of her top to stroke her waist, 'I'll aim for A plus with an excellence distinction.'

Her laugh banished the last of his doubts. Kat was an intelligent and beautiful woman who could have anyone. That she'd chosen to break such a long dry spell with him was incredibly flattering. And no one, especially not Kat, deserved to have their sexuality neglected for so long.

'Can we get naked now that we've set the parameters?' Amusement danced in her eyes.

'Absolutely.' He slid his hands up her ribs, bunching up her blouse and lifting it over her head.

In return, Kat urged his arms up, helping him to yank off his shirt. When she hummed appreciatively and pressed a kiss to his bare chest, he had to force himself to take things slow.

His body was primed for action, his stare was drawn to the curve of her breasts above the lace of her bra. But he was determined to worship every neglected inch of her body, make her feel as beautiful as she was physically.

Then on Monday they'd go back to being just colleagues. Neither of them needed the complication of a relationship. They could dispense with their powerful chemistry and move on, no regrets.

As if his brain had finally conceded power to his body, Grady dragged her closer, his elbows at her back and his hands tilting her face up to his kiss. Her breasts pressed against his chest, her hands roaming over his skin.

He walked her backwards towards the bed, where they stripped off their remaining clothes.

'There are condoms in the bathroom cabinet,' she said at the next chance he gave her to speak. 'Although,' she added with a nervous chuckle, 'we'll need to check the expiry date. They've been there a while, were a joke from one of my girlfriends.'

'I have one,' he reassured her, retrieving the protection from his wallet.

When he joined her back on the bed she slipped into his arms, her mouth back on his, their tongues once more duelling for satiation. He pressed her into the mattress, determined to take things slow, to make it good for Kat, who had waited a long time to trust her body with another man.

'You smell so good,' he groaned against her skin as he kissed a path down her neck and chest to her breast, taking the nipple into his mouth and lavishing the bud with swipes of his tongue.

Kat cried out, her nails digging into his shoulders.

'I have to taste all of you,' he said, scooting lower, his gaze roaming the curves of her astounding body, kissing her stomach and the silvery streak of her Caesarean section scar, her hipbones and finally in between her legs.

Kat gripped the sheets in her fists, her gasps of delight music to Grady's ears. They might only have this one night, but he'd make it count, make up for each year of her long abstinence. Take her trust in him and deliver on his promise.

Her orgasm, when it came, shook her like a rag doll, her cries echoing in the darkness as she gripped his hair as if for dear life and rode out every last spasm.

He gave her a few minutes to recover, kissing his way back up her body, her skin so sensitive she giggled more than once. Then he covered himself with a condom and lay beside her, self-satisfied warmth pounding through his veins.

'You're beautiful,' he said, cupping her face and drawing her mouth back to his, making sure that he'd kissed and caressed every part of her before he finally pushed inside her.

Grady had experienced lots of good sex, but there was something deeper about the connection between two pleasure-focused people sharing an honest and open connection. When he'd first met Kat he couldn't have predicted they'd have a single thing in common but as he drove them over the edge, his stare locked with hers, finishing with a hoarse cry of her name when she tumbled with him once more into blissful release, he knew for certain that his own love life had been severely short-changed.

* * *

Fortunately, Kat's box of condoms had still been in date.

'One last time,' Nash said, slipping inside her from behind.

'Yes,' Kat cried, curling her fingers into his hair and holding on tight. Needing more contact, she entwined her other hand with his where it lay flat against her stomach, her back melded to his front as they rocked together, desperate to make the pleasure of their one night last.

Nash too seemed reluctant to stop. It was as if, having set the rules, they were both determined to stretch out the experience beyond the realms of the space time continuum.

'Nash…' She'd said his name so many times in the past three hours she was almost hoarse from yelling it, screaming it, pleading for what, she didn't know. She'd never known anything like the passion they'd shared. He'd taken her in positions she'd never heard of, his thorough and inexhaustible form of sex the best she could have hoped for after six years of denial.

And she saw now that she'd forgone an essential part of her femininity after her heartbreak at the hands of Henry. Why had she waited so long? Except instinct told her that there was nothing common about this experience. Unlike his laid-back work persona, Nash was a perfectionist when it came to pleasure.

He cupped her breast, his thumb lazily swiping her now tender nipple. 'Don't leave it another six years, Kat.' His stubble grazed her neck, sending shivers down her spine. 'You deserve to be loved.'

She knew he meant physically, not emotionally. He couldn't possibly know that her deepest fear was that she was somehow unlovable because of Henry's rejection. But her eyes stung with the threat of tears all the same, a confusing mix of gratitude that she'd made the right decision in choosing Nash as a lover for the night, in trusting him with her body, and apprehension, because sex this good was going to be so hard to forget.

But forget it she must. Because trusting him with her body was one thing. Beyond that, even if they wanted more, which they didn't, she'd forgotten how to extend that trust to relationship-building.

Instead of second-guessing the guard she'd placed around her heart six years ago, Kat imagined exactly how she would face Nash the next time they had a shift together, knowing that, among all of his other strengths, he was an enthusiastic and considerate lover. A part of her already regretted crossing the line, inviting him into her bed, because she was one hundred per-cent certain, now that she'd experienced a night in Nash's arms, that the one night on which she'd insisted was not going to be enough.

Except it had to be. They'd agreed. She'd made the rules and he'd made certain she understood he was no more looking for a relation-ship than she was.

As if he sensed her distraction, he moved on top of her. His hands cupped her face as he pushed inside her once more, his lips coaxing hers in a soft, sensual kiss.

'Stop over-thinking,' he whispered, as if he knew the exact contents of her head. But that was insane. He couldn't know her fears and doubts. He'd simply learned almost all there was to know about her body in one single night, that was all.

'Just feel,' he said, driving her higher and higher, helping her to be free of her own head, making this one night so perfect a part of her wanted to never let him go.

Ignoring the dangerous inclination, she stared into his eyes, certain that she'd exhausted her body's supply of climaxes. But as sure as the morning sun was peeking over the horizon out-side, Nash kissed her and stroked her and drove into her until he'd dragged one more from her spent body, himself surrendering seconds later.

After he collapsed, Kat rolled onto her side, buried her face against his neck, swallowing the ridiculous urge to cry. She wasn't a crier. She was just overwhelmed on endorphins, high on too much good sex and not enough sleep.

A trickle of fear for Monday morning crawled over her skin. She would have to work extra hard to ignore him now, to treat him like any other colleague, to act as if everything was back to normal, as if she hadn't learned what turned him on and what he looked like naked.

'I'm going to go,' he said after a few minutes of holding her close.

'Sure.' She nodded, reluctantly slipping her hands from around his waist.

Time to get her game face on.

He pressed a kiss to her temple, stood and disappeared into the bathroom. When he emerged he was fully dressed. His hair was sex-rumpled and his stare sleepy. He looked hotter than ever and, worse, he'd shown her his vulnerable side tonight, confided in her about his marriage and his hopes for Molly, shown her that there was way more to him than the irresponsible charmer she'd first assumed. She wanted to drag this new-found version of him back to bed and suggest that he stay until morning, that they talk some more, get to know each other better, but that wasn't part of one-night stand protocol.

He bent over her, a knowing smile making him look more boyish. But he was one hundred percent man. She knew that now.

In an absurd display of belated modesty, because he'd seen and tasted every part of her, Kat clutched the sheet to her chest and his smile widened.

'That was the best birthday I've ever had,' he said, brushing his lips against hers, feather-soft.

It left her wanting more.

To hide the fact, she laughed, grateful to him for making light of the situation.

'Bye, Kat.' He pressed his lips to hers in a final kiss that was way too brief and left the room and then the house.

Deflated, her skin crawling with trepidation, Kat lay still for the longest time after she'd listened to his car pulling away, her overriding emotion in the face of such an overwhelming success perversely that of failure.

The younger Kat, newly graduated from medical school, who had travelled overseas on a big life adventure, the way most young New Zealanders did, had been full of optimism and hope. She'd fallen hard for Henry, had loved him deeply. But why, when he'd proved himself to be so unworthy of her love, unworthy of his beautiful and funny daughter, had she allowed him to tear down her confidence so completely?

Nash was right. Her personal life didn't have to be over just because of one mistaken choice, one sour relationship. Kat might have reached that conclusion earlier if her mistake hadn't also had long-reaching consequences for both Lucy's emotional wellbeing and her father's health.

Maybe if her error in judgement had only affected Kat, if *her* broken heart had been the only casualty, she might have overcome the betrayal more easily.

She rolled over and tugged the duvet up to her chin, for the first time since Henry considering that one day she might be able to move on. Of course, a relationship involved a lot more than one incredible night. But if she was brave enough to sleep with Nash, to listen to her body and admit that she had needs beyond work and motherhood, maybe she could be brave enough to start dating again, when the time was right.

She fell asleep, thanks to Nash her dreams full of possibilities.

CHAPTER EIGHT

THREE DAYS LATER, the first shift he and Kat shared since they'd slept together, Grady pushed open the door to the multi-bedded resuscitation bay to find her busy at one of the computer workstations. His blood surged at the sight of her—those lips that had tasted so addictive on Saturday night pursed in concentration, her expressive eyes downturned when in pleasure they'd glowed with golden embers as she'd clung to him, her hair tamed into a practical ponytail when he could still recall its scent and lush silkiness between his fingers and trailing over his skin.

He clenched his jaw. This obsession had to end. He was breaking the rules, exactly what she'd accused him of that first day they'd met. She'd been adamant it was for one night and he'd insisted on clear expectations.

So why was he so eager to have her look at him the way she had when he'd kissed her goodbye, as if he'd taken her to heaven and back? Was it just ego on his part? If so, he could get over that.

When she'd said they should pretend like it hadn't happened, he didn't realise she meant to act as if they were strangers, or the adversaries from her first day. But beyond her brief *Good morning* they hadn't spoken a word.

He should have felt relieved that she was *business as usual* at work, so much so that no one would suspect they were anything other than barely acquainted colleagues. Instead, he'd tied himself into knots considering what he truly wanted. Walking away from such great sex was, of course, difficult. But did he truly want his often perplexing personal life further stretched by a fling with a work colleague?

Molly took up all of his spare energy. She was his priority. And managing Carol also sapped his time and energy. Only yesterday she'd turned up on his doorstep unannounced, demanding to see Molly because she had an unexpected shift cancellation, when they were supposed to stick to their appointed custody days.

Irked that he was so emotionally labile when Kat—who had barely given him the time of day all morning—seemed to have reverted easily to their pre-sex distance, he cleared his throat.

'Your suspected meningitis case is almost here, Dr Collins.' His voice emerged a little gruffer than he would have liked. He didn't want Kat to know that he was having second thoughts about the one-night rule but the fact that she'd hardly registered his presence left him itchy with frustration, as if he'd been…used.

'Thanks,' Kat muttered, clearly focused on what she was doing. She seemed to be going out of her way to avoid any interaction with him, even professional courtesy.

Because he'd yet to move from the doorway, Kat looked up.

A flash of what looked like fear passed over her expression. 'Sorry, I'll be right with you.'

Her voice was clipped in a busy doctor-like fashion. Her attention returned to the monitor, making him aware he'd been effectively dismissed.

The hair at the back of his neck prickled.

Kat's behaviour reminded him of Carol. She'd walked all over his feelings during their short marriage, inconsiderate and focused on her own needs, her own agenda. And she was still trying to pull those kinds of stunts, even though she no longer had any claim to him.

He wasn't asking for much from Kat, just some eye contact would do. A small smile. Any sign that let him know that what they'd shared meant more to her than an item ticked off a to-do list.

Start new job—check
Socialise with work colleagues—check
Sleep with available man to break overly prolonged dry spell—check

Resentful that he should have listened to his doubts and never have slept with her, Grady locked open the double doors that separated Resus from the ambulance bay and made his way outside to receive their next patient.

As he watched the ambulance backing up he became aware of Kat arriving at his side. 'I think you can call me Kat, don't you?'

He glanced her way but she kept her eyes on the reversing vehicle.

She appeared breathless. Was she reacting to his proximity the way he couldn't help but react to hers? His arms could still feel her, the unique scent of her soft skin imprinted on his brain, her passionate moans as she'd called his name over and over looping through his head.

Had she any idea how hard it had been for him to leave her warm bed when his overriding desire had been to curl his body around hers and drift off to sleep with the beat of her heart thumping against his chest?

'Okay.' He clenched his jaw, desperate to get her alone and clear the air. 'Kat it is.'

He didn't play games. He didn't want tension at work. Better to talk about it, discuss how they felt, and then move on.

Only part of him was stuck. The last thing he'd been expecting when he'd found her in the car park behind The Har-Bar was that they'd end up in bed together. But despite the current ice queen vibe she was channelling for reasons only known to Kat, she'd not only opened up about Lucy's father, she'd been as insatiable for him as he'd been for her, one time leading to another and another until he'd been certain from the look of vulnerability in her eyes that she'd ask him to stay the night.

Shaking off the unsettling thought that he would have happily held Kat until it had been time to collect Molly from Carol's house, Grady jolted into action as the rear doors of the ambulance swung open.

Two paramedics wheeled out a stretcher carrying a little girl around Molly's age, her features pale underneath the oxygen mask on her face.

Work-focused, he guided the foot of the stretcher into Resus, aware of Kat's rapid stride at his side. The girl's concerned parents followed and Grady cast them what he hoped was a reassuring look. The girl was now in the best place, and hopefully he and Kat could assess and treat her quickly so that she was out of danger.

'This is Hannah Roberts,' the paramedic said as Kat and he transferred Hannah easily to the resus stretcher.

'She's a normally well six-year-old girl who's been ill with a fever for two days. This morning she became increasingly lethargic, with a worsening headache and vomiting,' the paramedic continued. 'Mum and Dad report what sounds like a seizure, with loss of consciousness lasting approximately two minutes.'

With his handover complete, the paramedic smiled reassuringly at Hannah and her parents and then left the family in their care.

Kat met Grady's stare, concern clear in her eyes.

Any confusion or regret fell away as they silently communicated. Meningitis, if not treated quickly, could be life-threatening. They both had daughters Hannah's age. They were obviously concerned about the worst-case scenario for this little girl. They could empathise with Hannah's parents, who must be terrified to see their daughter so seriously unwell.

Sadly, Grady recognised the helplessness from his personal experience during Molly's admissions for acute exacerbations of the asthma she'd had since she was three years old.

With a swallow Grady was certain only he witnessed, Kat prepared herself. She spoke to Hannah's parents in a calm, reassuring voice. While she took a more detailed history of events, Grady connected Hannah to various monitors that immediately began recording her vital signs. Relieved to see that the paramedic had applied local anaesthetic cream to the antecubital fossa of both arms, he set about obtaining venous access and extracted several vials of blood for the lab. Then, thinking ahead, he applied some more local anaesthetic cream to the little girl's lower back.

Kat would probably want to do a lumbar puncture.

Seeing his forethought, she nodded gratefully as she quickly examined Hannah.

The presentation was indeed worrying for meningitis. The sooner they could start some antibiotics, the sooner they could eliminate a life-threatening infection.

Grady brought up Hannah's hospital record on the computer and ordered the most likely blood tests he figured Kat would want, including blood cultures.

A few minutes later Kat joined him at the workstation, worry evident in her expression.

'What do you think?' he asked, his voice low so their conversation wouldn't be overheard. He had to fight the bizarre urge to smooth the frown creases between Kat's eyebrows with his fingertip. Instead, he concentrated on labelling each vial of blood for the lab.

'There's no rash,' said Kat, her voice betraying the tension she wore around her mouth, 'but she has photophobia and neck stiffness.'

That told Nash that Kat suspected the GP's diagnosis of meningitis was correct. The sooner they could administer the correct intravenous antibiotic, the better Hannah's chances were of fighting the infection.

'She needs a CT scan and an urgent lumbar puncture,' Kat said, sharing her concerns, their personal issues set aside while they focused on their patient.

He nodded. 'That's protocol in cases with this presentation.'

Her frown eased, as if she'd been waiting for his corroboration. 'Have you called the paediatrician? She'll need to be admitted.'

Grady winced, glancing over at where Hannah lay, still and worryingly uncomplaining, on the stretcher. He had no good news on that score.

He stepped closer, dropped his voice further. 'I informed the paeds team that we might have a meningitis case coming in as soon as I knew Hannah was on her way, but they're currently dealing with a SIDS case and Lauren is next door inserting a temporary pacemaker on a patient with symptomatic complete heart block.'

They stared at each other, the implications sinking in. For now, he and Kat were Team Hannah until the paediatrician was free. The emergency department often operated in a feast or famine way, one doctor or specialist needing to be in two places at once.

'You're experienced at lumbar punctures, right?' he asked, his expression as reassuring as he could make it. What he really wanted to do was hold her in his arms, feel her weight sink into him the way it had on Saturday, when she'd been open to him, trusting that he'd catch her when she fell apart.

She nodded, looking uncertain.

'Do you want me to talk to Lauren?' he offered. The department was busy as usual, but their acting head consultant would get Kat the supervision she needed, if required.

Kat nibbled at her lip. Then the doubt cleared. 'No, I've done it lots of times before.' She moved closer, her arm brushing his. 'It's just that... she's so little, you know.'

Nash nodded, compassion and concern a lump in his throat. He knew exactly what she was feeling. 'You're thinking of our girls?'

She nodded.

'Me too, for the record.' He gripped her arm above the elbow, giving her a light squeeze of encouragement. 'You can do this, Kat.'

Nash had watched her in action since her first day. He'd seen her dedication to patient care and her humility. She wasn't scared to ask for help when she needed it. If she said she could perform the lumbar puncture unsupervised he had complete faith in her.

As an ER doctor, she would have done the procedure many times before. Her second's wobble of confidence was solely down to maternal empathy.

Kat's eyes shone with gratitude. 'Yes, I can. Thanks, Nash.'

He nodded, dropping his hand from her arm and missing the contact immediately. 'I'll be right here to help if you need me. Do you want to prescribe some antibiotics so I can organise an IV infusion?'

She nodded and released a controlled sigh as she added her signature to the prescription. The smile she gave him spoke a thousand words. At work they could still operate as a team, even if they'd complicated their professional relationship by acting on their attraction and sleeping together.

Kat ordered the urgent CT scan and then spoke to Hannah and her parents, informing them that she needed to exclude meningitis with a lumbar puncture test.

Grady readied the equipment she'd need for the procedure. She didn't need him to hold her hand but he wanted to offer support in the same way he'd always mentored the junior doctors. That was how he and Lauren had become friends.

Except while they washed their hands side by side at the double sink Grady struggled to ignore the protective urges he felt towards Kat, aware that this felt more personal because they'd spent the night together. He should have known that sex was never just sex, especially when two people shared this kind of connection. Hopefully, there'd be time to talk about Saturday later.

Kat dried her hands and glanced over at Hannah once more. Their patient's age was understandably making her draw comparisons.

'You know,' he said as they put on sterile gloves, trying to ease their apprehension, 'Molly has asthma.'

Kat looked up, her shock turning to empathy.

'I've spent one or two nights here with her as an inpatient—longest nights of my life. But we both know that kids can be flat one minute and running around the ward chattering away the next.'

'I'm sorry to hear that about Molly,' she said, looking at him as if she wanted to touch him in a comforting way. Instead, she drew local anaesthetic into a syringe. 'You're right, children are resilient. Hopefully those antibiotics will work soon.'

The lumbar puncture procedure went smoothly. As Grady cleared away the used equipment, Kat's pager sounded, a call to assist one of the house officers with another case.

'I'll be back shortly,' she said, peeling off her gloves.

He nodded, glad that when it counted they could remain professional.

'I really appreciate your support.' A small smile twitched her mouth, one he recognised from Saturday when she'd looked at him as if he was the man of her dreams. Only he didn't want that. He just wanted more than the frosty distance of this morning.

'Any time,' he said, faking the easygoing vibe that before Kat had always come naturally. Now, his stomach was tight with anticipation, his reasoning conflicted, his precious certainties, the convictions he'd lived by since his divorce, rattled.

He watched her leave, his confusion proof that he was in danger where Kat was concerned.

CHAPTER NINE

FORTY MINUTES LATER, with a stable Hannah transferred to the neighbouring X-ray department for a CT scan, Kat entered the deserted staffroom, dragging in her first deep breath of the day.

Despite the reviving oxygen in her system, her hands trembled as she prepared a cup of coffee, the adrenaline only partly due to treating a seriously ill little girl the same age as Lucy.

Her remaining tremors were entirely related to Nash. The minute she'd seen him that morning every stern lecture she'd given herself over the weekend since they'd slept together might as well have been in a foreign language for all the sense it made to her shaky resolve. She'd insisted on their one-night rule for a reason: she neither wanted nor was ready for more.

Her long physical recovery from a difficult pregnancy and birth had been compounded by the emotional impact of Henry's cruel rejection. Her subsequent guilt over her father's stroke, helping to care for him while raising Lucy, meant that by the time she'd met Nash she'd almost forgotten how to interact with a man she found attractive.

Only despite the rules she'd laid down one night with Nash had unleashed a torrent of emotions. Kat had spent most of the weekend following her routines—walking on the beach with her parents and Lucy, visiting the farmers' market and shopping for groceries, tackling the week's laundry—trying to keep a lid on the way he'd made her feel beautiful, desired, more than just a mum.

No wonder it was taking all of her energy to walk that fine line between acting *normal* at work and wanting to drag him somewhere private, kiss him again and beg him to throw her rulebook out of the window so they could prolong their fling.

Aware of how erratic her emotions were, she sighed as she took a seat. Could Nash see how conflicted she was? Her cool as a cucumber act was probably convincing no one. But Nash was a reasonable man. Surely he could see that the sooner they returned to business as usual and dispensed with all the uncomfortable silences and stilted interactions the better for them both. They had jobs to do and busy personal lives.

If they could get past the awkwardness they'd be fine.

Gulping her coffee in the hope that the caffeine would straighten out her convoluted thoughts, Kat chided herself for her silly hormonal angst and forced her thoughts back to Hannah. The distress on the faces of her poor parents as Kat had put a needle into Hannah's lower spine to retrieve a sample of cerebrospinal fluid for testing haunted Kat.

She was so highly strung that without Nash's calming presence she might have embarrassed herself with the tears that threatened if she envisioned Lucy lying on a stretcher with a potentially life-threatening infection.

Nash's stoicism, given Molly's asthma, was humbling. Her respect for him had doubled.

Her body flooded with heat. No matter how hard she tried to wipe Saturday from her mind, all roads led back to Nash.

The staffroom door opened at Kat's back. Aware that she was no longer alone, she slapped a bright smile on her face and turned.

It was Nash.

'Oh…hi,' she said, her cheeks flushing, the frozen smile on her face more of an embarrassed grimace. Would he know that she'd spent the past three days fantasising about him? Could he sense the loneliness gnawing away inside her like a toothache, made stronger by his attention and compliments, which she'd soaked up like a sponge? She should never have slept with him in the first place. Because, just like it was impossible to stuff a champagne cork back inside the bottle, forgetting his touch, his kisses, his whispered words after such a long drought was impossible.

'Hi,' Nash said, his expression telling her that this morning's awkwardness was back.

He moved to the sink and Kat's brain turned to mush, all the things she wanted to say to him, things she'd spent the weekend practising and perfecting, vanished, the way they had when he'd walked into the resus room looking sexier than ever. The only thing left in her mind was, *I know we agreed it was a one-time thing, but you seem to have awoken the sex maniac in me. Want to do it again?*

Of course he didn't. He could barely look at her.

Kat blinked away the sting in her eyes, hoping that by selfishly sleeping with him she hadn't ruined their already fragile working relationship. She held her breath while Nash kept his back to her, preparing a drink. What she wouldn't give for the return of easygoing, rule-bending Nash. But without the buffer of a patient, or unless it was physical, they seemed to have forgotten how to interact with each other.

Nash glanced over his shoulder, their stares colliding.

'Would you like to be alone?' he asked, his voice infuriatingly relaxed as if this was one of their pre-sex conversations. 'I can sit in the corner and pretend that we haven't seen each other, if you want.'

Kat bristled, annoyed that he was calm enough to make jokes and that he seemed to be implying the issue lay solely with her.

'Don't be ridiculous. We don't have to ignore each other.' Although it might help her hormonal imbalance if he promised to forget how she looked naked. Lord help her...even now she was still trying to scrub his gloriously male physique from her mind.

'Don't we?' he said, his stare seeming to probe every last one of the scars Henry had inflicted on her ability to trust both her own judgement and romantic relationships in general. 'Apart from when we've had to set our issues aside for the sake of our patients, it seems to me that you'd prefer to pretend that I didn't exist. I know we said we'd ignore the fact that we had sex, but ignoring each other is taking it too far.'

Kat's indignation soared along with her body

temperature at his casual mention of the sex. Her eyes darted around the staffroom, checking they were still alone. 'I wasn't ignoring you; I was just trying to follow the rules,' she hissed, 'trying to behave professionally at work.'

Of course he wouldn't appreciate her efforts. Of course he would be the first one to disregard the guidelines they'd both put in place in order to move on from the best sex Kat had ever had.

'I'd expect nothing less,' he muttered, stirring his coffee and clattering the teaspoon into the sink.

'I suppose you'd rather we discuss it blow by blow, would you?' she asked, determined to act as casually as him.

Oh, please let him decline. A detailed post-mortem of the experience might tip her over the edge.

'And to think,' she said, 'that I'd been about to thank you for being such a gentleman by not mentioning it.' To stop the bubble of hysterical laughter that threatened to erupt, she took another scalding sip of coffee. They were acting worse than their five-year-olds.

As if he too saw the ridiculous in their squabbling, Nash grinned, added a splash of milk to his coffee and then took the seat next to hers.

Kat wanted to squirm at the chaos his closeness was causing in both her head and her pelvis. How could he simultaneously turn her on and rile her up?

Leaning into her personal space, he stage-whispered, 'Who said I was a gentleman?'

His gaze held her captive, every second he stared, his eyes full of intimate knowledge of the night they'd shared, pulsing through her weak body.

She ignored his question. His integrity was part of the reason she'd trusted him with her body in the first place.

'See,' he continued, his deep voice low and conspiratorial in a way that made her pulse sky-rocket, 'you don't know the real me at all.'

Was that what bothered him? Was he offended that she'd tried—and failed, although she wouldn't be confessing that—to forget their one-night stand? Of course she wanted to get to know Nash better, beyond his skills as a lover. But even though Henry and Nash couldn't be more different, she was still struggling to trust her judgement when it came to the opposite sex.

'I may not know everything about you,' she said, hoping he couldn't hear the longing in her voice, 'but I know that for some reason you're trying to get a rise out of me.'

And she was taking the bait.

Infuriating man. Why couldn't they just move

on from the fact they'd slept together and go back to being colleagues?

Because she still wanted to rip his clothes off, that was why. He shifted in his seat, getting comfortable, the move bringing them so close their arms brushed, heightened physical awareness prickling her skin as if she was allergic to her scrubs. Kat tried to scoot as far away from him as the chair would allow, but it was too late. The memories of his weight on top of her, his stubble grazing her neck, the mindless passion of his kisses rushed her mind.

'And I know that you're most likely prickly out of fear,' he replied, casually sipping his drink.

'Fear?' she huffed.

Confident, Nash nodded slowly. 'Yes, you're scared to get to know me because you've spent years being closed-off.'

'I'm not closed-off.' Kat gaped, outraged because he could see through her so effortlessly. Ever since that night she seemed to be entirely composed of emotions. Just like the sex, it had been six years since she'd trusted anyone enough to show them her softer side. 'Just because I made the mistake of thinking you'd respect my rules, that we could move on from what happened on Saturday.'

If only she could move on.

Her body was desperate for more, although it would have to go back to surviving without regular sex. She stood a small chance of forgetting one time, if only Nash would stop looking at her as if he'd taken mental photographs. But indulging more than once meant getting to know him, opening up, being vulnerable— exactly what she feared the most.

How did he know?

'Well, one of us had to raise the topic.' He pursed his lips to blow the surface of his coffee.

Kat swallowed hard, reminded of his kisses, of all the places those lips had explored. Was he enjoying making her feel hot and bothered in good ways and bad?

'Why do we have to talk about it at all?' she implored. 'Can't we just forget it happened, as agreed?'

His eyes flashed with sympathy, his stare dipping to her mouth. 'I don't really want to forget the best birthday I've ever had.'

Kat opened her mouth, words failing her as she remembered how he'd held her with such tenderness, how he'd whispered things he hadn't needed to say.

Why was he changing the rules, and why was a part of her tempted to do the same?

'Look, Kat,' he said, his voice gentle, 'I guess I am technically breaking one of the rules by raising the subject, but I guess I'd hoped you might be interested in getting to know me better, at least at work.'

She wanted that. Why hadn't she suggested it first?

'I'll be honest,' Nash continued. 'This morning I couldn't help but feel that you used me for sex, only to put me back on the shelf like some sort of toy.'

Kat gasped, appalled. 'That's not true.'

Was it? Had her attempt to put the best sex of her life behind her, as promised, made him feel used? When it came to men, she'd had her guard up for so long she wore it like a second skin. Could it be that made her appear cold and egotistical, uncaring of how Nash might feel?

'It feels true from where I'm standing.' He placed his half-drunk coffee on the table. 'If I'd had your number I'd have called you on Sunday to clear the air, make sure you were okay. I've waited all morning for this opportunity to get you alone. But when I walked in just now you looked like you wanted to run.'

Kat flushed, shame burning her cheeks, because a part of her had wanted to flee. She was so confused over her expectations—having one night of pleasure and putting it behind her—and reality, waking up on Sunday morning flooded with feelings she hadn't experienced in years, with the yearning for more of Nash gnawing in the pit of her stomach, that she'd totally freaked out.

'I… I just…' Dropping her head, she groaned silently. He was right. She was inflexible and closed-off and afraid.

She'd set aside her own needs when she'd limped away from Henry, focused on motherhood, her job, repaying her parents for their support. It was easier to set that part of herself aside than to probe the way that her ex had made her feel not good enough.

Reeling, she blurted the truth. 'I'm sorry that you feel used. I'm just not used to putting my needs first the way I did on Saturday and, if I'm brutally honest, I wasn't expecting it to be that good. I became completely overwhelmed.' She looked away from the compassion that filled his stare, embarrassed by her sad admission. She didn't want to be so transparent.

'I'm struggling to forget it myself,' he said, that sexy smile of his making a reappearance.

Kat nodded, looked away, forced herself to lower her guard. 'But I'm not looking for a relationship. Lucy's father threw me away like rubbish and for a long time I felt like there must be something wrong with me.'

'There isn't,' he said emphatically.

'I know, but just because we had sex doesn't

mean trust comes automatically. I'm processing a lot, so I'm sorry if I handled it badly. I told you that I was rusty.'

A small frown settled between his brows. 'I'm sorry that you were so badly let down, but I'm not interested in hurting you, Kat. I'm not that guy. That's why I made certain our expectations aligned before we slept together. I'm not looking for a relationship either.'

'I know.' Kat nodded, her cheeks hot. 'You're considerate and understanding and honourable. I'm not used to that.' He wasn't Henry, she understood that on an intellectual level, but her subconscious fears clearly had no such insight, maybe because it wasn't just her happiness at stake any more. There was Lucy to consider.

On Saturday night he'd made her feel cared for—ensuring she was safe when he'd discovered her stranded in the car park, escorting her to her dark front door, telling her she was beautiful and catching her as she'd fallen apart.

Peeking at him from under her lashes, she smiled, feeling raw and exposed. 'I guess I practised the rules too diligently, overdid the casualness.'

'It's okay.' He shrugged. 'I probably overreacted, a side-effect of the divorce.'

Kat nodded, curious for more but emotionally wrung-out. 'So what now?'

They still had the same priorities: their girls and work. As he'd just reminded her, he was no more interested in a relationship than she was.

He tilted his head, a hint of regret in his eyes. 'We go back to your rules.'

Kat nodded, while her stomach sank. She'd voiced the rules to keep herself from getting hurt again, but she couldn't help her stab of disappointment that neither of them was willing to risk more than one night, when it had been Nash's rule-bending that had first brought him to her attention.

'Good plan,' Kat croaked, staring at her hands in her lap.

'If it helps, we should get to know each other better,' he said, as if in consolation. 'As you pointed out that day in the playground, it makes sense for us to be friends, because Molly is smitten with Lucy.'

Kat's heart lurched at the vulnerability in his stare when he mentioned his daughter, just like when he'd shared Molly's medical history earlier.

'That's exactly what I want too.' She forced a bright smile. Friends was okay as consolation prizes went, although him being a complete jerk would help her to dismiss the sex her body still craved.

The last thing she needed was a sexy male

friend/colleague she couldn't look at without being assaulted by erotic memories, especially when, despite all of the fears he'd recognised in her, he'd also awoken some long-buried emotional vault she owed it to herself to explore.

'Good,' he said, sounding far from convinced as he scanned her expression.

'That's sorted then,' she replied, unable to break the eye contact that had somehow gone on way too long for people negotiating a mere friendship.

'Perfect,' Nash said, his gaze sliding to her lips, settling there, searching as if he were testing the credibility of her resolve.

Kat held her breath. He couldn't be. He'd just confirmed that he was happy with the rules. Except when his eyes met hers once more they carried the flare of heat she'd seen time and time again on Saturday night.

Was he going to kiss her again?

Her pulse flew. He was going to kiss her again.

Her bones started to melt, the taste of his lips already on hers as if they'd been kissing nonstop since their first time on her doorstep.

His pager bleeped. He scanned the screen and stood, his expression clear, so that Kat wondered if she'd imagined the sexual tension. 'Hannah is back from her CT scan.'

Kat's endorphin high plummeted as he placed his mug in the dishwasher, seemingly unaffected by the past few seconds.

Kat nodded, dumbfounded by how quickly he could veer from heated looks that seemed to speak louder than actual words to work-focused and how easily led her body had proved.

'I'll…um speak to Paediatrics,' she said, her voice husky with arousal, 'see how long before we can get her admitted.'

Forget friends. Her body wanted to stride across the staffroom, tug the neck of his scrubs and finish what he'd started with his eyes moments ago.

Instead, she cleared her dry throat. 'Let me know when the lumbar puncture results come through.'

'Will do.'

He left the staffroom, where Kat tried to reassemble the pieces of her scattered wits, slipping easily back into old patterns of self-denial.

CHAPTER TEN

THE FOLLOWING SATURDAY Grady knocked at the red front door where the six-year-old's party was being held, a big smile at the ready so he didn't display any of his uncertainties to Molly. He glanced down at his daughter, relieved to see her happy and so excited that she couldn't keep still.

Despite the positive signs, his stomach pinched with nerves. She looked adorable dressed as a princess, but he couldn't stave off the trepidation that he'd somehow messed up Molly's outfit.

After all, what did a six-foot-three ex-soldier like him know about princesses?

Not for the first time, he questioned that his efforts as a solo dad were enough for his daughter. He'd left the army before Molly was born, as soon as Carol had begun making noises about pursuing a new career in the airline industry. Sometimes he missed the camaraderie and varied work of his old career. Although at the time he'd consoled himself that Molly had needed stability and consistency.

He still feared that she might need a more dependable female influence, especially on days like today.

Interrupting his pity party that, through the choices he and Carol had made, they were letting down their beautiful girl, the front door swung open and the host mum appeared, surrounded by a parade of similarly dressed princesses all craning their necks to assess the new arrival.

'Hi,' Grady said to the woman, gripping Molly's hand tighter. 'This is Molly and I'm Nash Grady, her dad.'

He was so out of his depth that his palms were sweating.

Molly smiled sweetly and handed over their wrapped gift to another princess that Grady presumed was the birthday girl. Squeals of excitement ensued among the princesses.

To his utter relief, Lucy appeared, immediately taking Molly's free hand.

As if attuned to her presence, he glanced into the hallway, instantly spying Kat, who was looking down, manoeuvring her way out through the animated throng.

The sight of her triggered a cascade of testosterone in his blood. His heart jerked an erratic rhythm in his chest the way it had when he'd almost caved and kissed her in the staff-room after they'd both admitted that one time hadn't been enough.

He'd been so tempted to suggest another hook-up but he didn't want to hurt her the way she'd been hurt before, so instead they'd decided on friendship.

As if hearing his internal groan of frustration, Kat looked up. Their eyes met. Static buzzed in Grady's head, the chatter of children and words of the host fading.

Damn, she looked good, her face relaxed and her hair free of its practical work ponytail. She smiled, the hesitant but intimate smile he both loved and dreaded. He could be her friend. It made sense for both of them to avoid further complications.

Nope, sense was overrated. He just wanted to barge past the five and six-year-olds and kiss Kat again until he'd reminded her how good they'd been together.

Aware that he was staring, he looked away as Kat finally managed to exit the front door to join him on the doorstep.

'Have a fun time, okay?' he said to Molly, stooping to her level for a final check that she was a happy little princess.

She barely acknowledged her hovering father,

clearly desperate to get inside and hurl herself into the party action. But just as she stepped over the threshold, side by side with Lucy, her tiara slipped from her head onto the ground.

Grady bent to retrieve it at the exact same moment as Kat. Their hands collided, hers a fraction of a second ahead of his.

'Oops, here you go,' she said, holding her prize out to Molly, who simply stood dutifully in front of Kat, her face regally upturned as if she wore a crown every day and was used to the attention of ladies-in-waiting.

Before he could step in and fix it—although he'd been the one responsible for precariously fitting the slippery apparel in the first place—Kat replaced the tiara on Molly's head, expertly fastening it in place with the stabby little side combs that had almost given Grady an aneurysm.

He exhaled a sigh of relief as the girls trotted inside, followed by an already slightly frazzled-looking host. He was overreacting. Molly looked like all the other little girls, the outfit he'd sweated over appropriate. She even appeared none the worse for having been dressed by a man who'd spent way too long on the internet researching tiaras versus crowns. He'd almost called Kat several times for dress-up advice.

That was the kind of things friends did, right?

The door closed, leaving them alone on the doorstep. He swallowed, recalling another doorstep, passionate kisses, a night he'd never wanted to end.

'Thanks,' he said, 'for fixing the tiara. It took me ages to put it on. Clearly there's a knack I need to master.' And master it he would. He wouldn't have Molly feeling different because her mother was rarely in the picture.

'They fall off all the time.' Kat smiled, her tinkle of laughter boosting his confidence that, despite knowing his way around an assault rifle, he wasn't as terrible as he feared when it came to princess costumes.

'I'm sure they are going to have lots of fun,' Kat said, glancing back at the closed door.

'I hope so. She's so excited; she's been awake since six this morning,' Grady said, grateful that Lucy and Molly's friendship seemed unwavering. At first he'd wondered if Molly's obsession with Lucy would be a flash in the pan, but all he heard when she was at home was *Lucy does this* and *Lucy said that*.

'Lucy too.' Kat laughed as they walked back to the pavement together.

Did he imagine her checking him out?

His own thoughts were seriously un-platonic.

Want to book into a motel for an hour and

see if last Saturday was a fluke? How about an amendment to the former rule—just friends at work, lovers in our own time?

At his car, which was parked on the street, Kat hesitated. 'Do you have plans…?' she said, all trace of the awkwardness from the other day gone. 'I was going to grab some coffee. There's a place nearby.' She pointed in the direction of the beach, which was a few streets' walk away.

'If by plans you mean going home to tackle the week's laundry, I'd love some coffee.'

With the exception of Molly, he couldn't think of anyone else he'd rather spend time with at the moment.

See, he could do friends.

They set off walking. The day was warm. Kat wore a loose short-sleeved shirt, through which he spied distracting glimpses of bra, and cut-off denim shorts that made her backside and tanned legs look so amazing he almost walked into a lamppost.

'So, I've been thinking…' She glanced his way, her expressive eyes concealed by her sunglasses, her sensual mouth set in that determined line he'd come to recognise.

For the millionth time since their conversation in the staffroom he wondered why he hadn't just come out and told her that any time she needed to scratch an itch she could use him as much as she liked.

'Oh?' Insanely attracted to Kat, he'd been so wary of rushing into a fling after that spectacular night, hung up on past resentment that Carol hadn't really known him, otherwise she wouldn't have found him constantly lacking during their marriage, that he'd not only hammered home his message on keeping things casual, he'd also insisted on the *friends* thing. When all he really wanted was to put that satiated look on her face over and over again.

Kat snorted. 'You were right about getting to know each other so, in that spirit, I'd like to know something new about you every time we speak. What do you think?' She flicked a triumphant smile his way, shoving her sunglasses on top of her head.

That in this moment he'd quite happily be her plaything. Was it too late to ask if the rules he'd agreed to uphold were negotiable?

'It doesn't have to be personal,' she said, assuming he needed convincing. 'I'm just trying to redress the balance of what I know about… you…you know…physically.'

Man, she was adorable when she blushed.

The trouble was that his desire for her hadn't abated one little bit. If anything, it was growing stronger the more time they spent working together. Since they'd cleared the air, Kat had often sought him out with a work-related question, joking around with him the way she did with the other nurses. It was as if, slowly but surely, day by day, she was letting a little more of her guard slip.

He'd taken to leaving doors open every time they were alone to stop himself from suggesting they pick up where they'd left off the night of his birthday.

No, this was better. They had too much in common to ruin it with sex.

'So, what do you think?' she asked as they crossed the road.

Realising that she was waiting for an answer and that what he truly thought was in no way fit for admitting aloud, he cleared his throat. 'I think it's a great idea.'

'Good.' She nodded, looking pleased. 'It's obvious that our girls are determined to be best friends. So we're probably going to be seeing a lot more of each other outside of work.'

He smiled, held the door open and followed her into the café. He should have been more careful about his wishes. She was enough of a temptation at the hospital with people around and no hope of anything physical taking place. But spending more time outside of work, focused on getting to know each other... He'd need to invest in a straitjacket to keep his hands to himself.

They ordered drinks and sat outside, his rejuvenated libido imagining play dates between Molly and Lucy as an excuse to see Kat.

'Are you okay?' she asked. 'You seemed stressed earlier.'

Grady rubbed his hand over his chin and the days' worth of stubble there, nodding. 'I just had a dad/daughter freak-out about the party. I don't want Molly to feel different because her father doesn't know one end of a fairy wand from the other.'

'Oh, stop.' She narrowed her eyes with mock censure. 'You're a great dad and you know it.'

Her compliment shifted something inside his chest. Did he know that? He certainly tried his best to give Molly as good an upbringing as his single mother had given him, but most days he felt as if he was running around extinguishing fires armed only with a water pistol.

He sighed, lamenting how little he could rely on Carol for help. 'You have no idea how relieved I was to see all the other girls dressed similarly to Molly.'

'Didn't Carol help?' she asked, and he realised that this was what friends did. They chatted, confided, shared, just like he'd inadvertently forced Kat to open up about her trust issues.

Sighing, he shook his head. 'It's officially her weekend to have Molly, but I haven't heard from her.' Not unusual when his ex had a new man in her life or if work took her somewhere exotic for days on end.

'Does she do that a lot? Let you and Molly down?' Kat asked, frowning.

He shrugged in answer. 'I couldn't care less for myself. I love every minute I spend with Molly.' He parented alone just fine, as did Kat.

'But you love Molly enough that you want her to have a relationship with her mother.' Her eyes brimmed with understanding.

'Even when it sometimes means I'm literally giving her chance after chance to let Molly down. I know. I can't win.'

'Do you mind me asking what happened with you two to cause the divorce?' Her teeth scraped her bottom lip and Grady once more thought of her passionate kisses and the way she'd cast aside all of her barriers when they'd been intimate.

If only she showed that side of herself more often, but then he couldn't blame her for being cautious. He was himself after rushing into marriage, giving up his career, watching it all crumble.

He owed it to Molly, if to no one else, to keep his relationships casual.

'Carol and I were never right for each other,' he said, exhaling the tension this subject caused. If Kat could open up, he could too. 'We met while I was still an army medic. I think Carol hoped for an exciting life of overseas postings in exotic places, but we'd only known each other a few months when she fell pregnant.' He shrugged, an indulgent smile twitching his mouth at the memory of holding his newborn little girl for the first time, how he'd marvelled at her minuscule fingernails and the sooty length of her eyelashes.

'Failed birth control,' he clarified, although a part of him had suspected Carol had planned the *oops* to encourage a proposal, as it indeed had. Not that he was free from responsibility—it took two to make a baby and what an adorable one he and Carol had created together. Grady had been instantly and eternally smitten.

'So you proposed,' Kat said, a look of fascination in her eyes.

He shrugged just as the waitress appeared with their drinks. He took a grateful sip before continuing. 'Yeah. It felt like the right thing to do at the time. I was excited about becoming a dad. So we got married, I left the army and took a job at Gulf Harbour and Molly was born. For a while I felt as if I'd won the lottery. Then everything began turning sour.'

'In what way?' Kat asked, her sympathetic stare encouraging him to continue.

'I don't think Carol really wanted her single life to be changed by parenthood. Even before Molly was born she announced plans to retrain as a flight attendant. Nothing I did was good enough—I didn't earn enough money, or I worked too hard, or we never did anything exciting.'

He grimaced, surprised anew by the familiar taste of defeat that had been a constant during their marriage. 'I was raised by a single parent. My mother did her hardest to make sure I didn't feel disadvantaged, but I was determined that my child would have the best of everything, including two parents in a committed relationship. But that's not how it turned out.'

'I'm sorry that it didn't work out, but don't take all of the blame on yourself.'

Grady shrugged, his heart thudding faster when she seemed to see things about him it had taken years for him to see himself. 'I did blame myself for a while. But I don't think my ex really wanted me specifically, rather she wanted someone committed to her and I fit the bill. But where I was content to spend the weekends doing family stuff—walks in the park, fixing up the house, cooking—Carol became increasingly restless, always out for drinks or celebrating something with her new work friends, or planning girls' holidays with the staff discounted air tickets.'

Kat waited patiently, her barely touched coffee cooling in front of her.

'Once resentment sets into a marriage it's like rot,' he said. 'It spreads, and no amount of glue can hold it together. I didn't want our wonderful daughter to be that glue, so I suggested a trial separation in the hope that Carol would realise what she had and rush back to us with fresh perspective. But the opposite happened.'

He'd failed to create a happy family of his own. He'd let Molly down.

'Did she meet someone else?' Kat asked, her voice quiet, her eyes full of compassion.

He shrugged. 'She started dating a series of pilots as if Molly and I didn't exist. Rather than feel betrayed, I realised that I was happier without her, that just like she'd seen something in me that wasn't there—some macho tough-guy solider who would sweep her off her feet and provide a life of thrills with none of the mundane moments—I hadn't really known her either. I'd just rushed to do the right thing as I saw it by proposing.'

He shrugged again, taking a mouthful of coffee so he didn't say any more.

'You know,' she said, leaning forward so her elbows rested on the table, 'Molly is a lovely little girl. You should be very proud of her. You're doing a great job, and I can say that because I know how hard it is raising a child alone. She still has two parents and it's probably better for her to know you both happy on your own than together but full of resentment.' She held his stare, her understanding dissolving some of his worries for Molly.

Single parents faced extra challenges, but that didn't mean they weren't doing their best to be everything a child needed. Kat pursued her career, studied for her professional exams and made sure she was always there for Lucy.

Grady nodded, now almost desperate with curiosity about the man who had abandoned a woman like Kat. 'What about you? Tell me about Lucy's father.'

It was Kat's turn to shrug, to shift in her seat as if mildly uncomfortable. 'I think of him as a sperm donor actually, because being a father is what you do for Molly, not just donating genes.'

To try and banish the sadness in her eyes, Grady reached across the table and took her hand, squeezed her fingers. 'I'm sorry. You don't have to talk about it. Forget I asked.'

Kat shook her head, determination in her

stare. She held his hand, silent communication passing between them so he felt her trust like a hesitant caress.

'It's okay. I met him on my OE,' she said about the overseas experience, a working holiday considered a rite of passage by most young New Zealanders. 'I was so full of optimism, a qualified doctor, living in London. I felt invincible.'

Grady smiled, imagining a younger Kat taking on the world.

'Stupidly, I fell in love, swept off my feet by a charmer, as it turned out.' She fiddled with her teaspoon, swirling it idly through the foam on her coffee, disrupting what was left of the barista's artwork. 'Lucy's father had that X-factor, you know, had this way of making you feel like you were the only person on the planet.' She huffed. 'And I fell for it…'

'I see.' He waited, his sympathy pulsing with each beat of his heart. Her pain made him want to book the first flight to London and hunt this guy down.

'He made all these promises,' she continued, 'all the things we'd do together, all the places we'd travel and the amazing life we'd have. I was working every minute that I didn't spend with him, surviving on little or no sleep. I must have inadvertently missed a couple of pills because, the next thing I knew, I was expecting Lucy.'

When she looked up the love he saw shining in her eyes almost stole his breath.

'He was a mistake, but my darling girl is a wonderful gift.'

Grady nodded in understanding. Their core values were so similar. How had he ever considered them opposites?

'I was so excited,' she said. 'I loved my career, but I also hoped to have a family one day. When I told Henry that I was having our baby, at first he was shocked but supportive. Then, quite literally overnight, he changed, became distracted and less attentive. As the weeks went by, he was increasingly hard to pin down, avoiding my calls and making excuses for why he was too busy to see me.'

Her expression hardened. 'I'm not stupid. I heard the message. When I confronted him, told him that our baby was coming whether he wanted to face it or not, said we needed a grown-up conversation about becoming parents, he showed his true colours. He informed me that I was being irresponsible, selfish, that I'd made the decision to have our baby alone so I could raise it alone, and he left, just like that.'

Grady stiffened, stunned. 'I can't believe it.' He tried to hide the worst of his shock for Kat's sake.

She nodded, the humiliation in her eyes confirmation. 'He's never met Lucy, despite me leaving him my New Zealand contact info before I left London.'

Grady stroked his thumb over the back of her hand, desperate to hold her until the vulnerability in her voice faded.

'The worst part,' she said, glancing away, 'is that my mistake…it affects other people, just like he said.'

Grady frowned, drawing her eyes back to his with a small tug on her hand. 'Who? Lucy? I hate that this guy let both of you down so casually, but she's better off without a father like that.'

Kat inhaled a shuddering breath. 'Not just her,' she whispered.

He waited, hoping that she'd tell him more so he could contradict the guilt she'd clearly heaped on her own shoulders.

'When I returned from the UK I moved back in with my parents. I don't think I'd have made it without them. I had a miserable pregnancy, complicated by pre-eclampsia and an emergency Caesarean section.'

Grady sighed. 'That's an awful lot to go through alone, Kat.'

She didn't acknowledge his comment, only gnawed at her lip and continued. 'To complicate matters, my father had a stroke shortly after Lucy was born. I'm glad I was there to help out with his rehabilitation, but I can't help but think the stress of having his single pregnant daughter back home, what with all of my complications, must have contributed to Dad's stroke.'

Words failed him. He shook his head automatically. 'You're being hard on yourself. It sounds like a terrible time for all of you. You can't take responsibility for everything.'

No wonder her ex's rejection had created deep-seated trust issues. Kat was intelligent and caring. She'd hate to think that a choice she'd made had impacted on others.

Kat peered up at him from beneath her lashes. 'I hate that he might have been right, that I was irresponsible.'

'By doing the right thing for you?' Grady asked. 'By being a great mother and an amazing doctor? He just didn't want to accept his share of the responsibility so he heaped it all on you and walked away.'

He hated that she looked uncertain.

'After that, I felt as if it took me the first two years of Lucy's life to recover, both physically and emotionally.' She shot him a tentative smile. 'And, of course, I was also trying to find a new job that would employ a frazzled single mother who often wasn't sure what day of the week it was.'

As if spent, she took a long swallow of coffee. 'Do you think you'll ever give marriage another try?' she asked from behind her coffee cup.

Dazed from everything he'd learned about her, Grady frowned. 'I don't know, to be honest. Molly has been let down enough. You saw on the first day of school that she's old enough to understand people coming and going from her life.' The handful of casual dates he'd had since his divorce had been nothing special. Sex was one thing, but making another woman a part of his and Molly's lives, the potential for disruption and disaster... She would need to be an exceptional woman to warrant the risk.

Kat nodded in agreement, finally releasing his hand to place her cup carefully back on the saucer. 'That's why I've totally neglected that side of my life too.' She flushed.

Was she remembering their night? It was never far from his mind.

They finished their coffees, talk turning to easier topics: their girls, the school programme for the term, the upcoming swimming lessons. Baffled by what he'd learned, his attraction to

Kat stronger than ever, he half participated in the conversation, half grappled with his shifting feelings.

He respected Kat, he wanted to obey her rules and be her friend, but she deserved so much more than she'd been dealt by Lucy's father. Any man would be lucky to have her. She was hard on herself when all she'd done was fall for the wrong man—his problem, not hers. Surely that justified one little bend of the rules?

'Thanks for suggesting coffee,' he said, pausing in the shade of a tree outside the café. 'I'm glad we had that talk.' Glad, but more conflicted than ever.

Kat looked up at him, her lips parted distractingly. 'You're welcome.'

His pulse pounded in his head. He didn't want to ruin what they had, but nor could he seem to fight their chemistry. 'I know what my thing is,' he said, catching the way her breathing sped up.

It was still there, the pull, the mutual consciousness, the compatibility.

She frowned, her lips pursed in confusion.

'The new thing that you don't already know,' he added, hoping to fill her head with something other than the worthless ex who'd hurt her so badly she hadn't gone near another man for six years.

'Oh. What?' She looked as if she were holding her breath.

He stepped closer, couldn't help himself. 'I want you to know that if this were a date, which it isn't, because dating isn't a priority for either of us—'

Kat licked her lips, her pupils dilating as she gave an impatient nod.

'And if I'd chosen a better place for this conversation than this spot next to the bins…' He paused, his gaze tracing the curve of her mouth. 'I would very much want to break your rules and kiss you again right now.'

She swallowed, her shocked speechlessness lasting the entire walk back to the party.

CHAPTER ELEVEN

BY THE FOLLOWING FRIDAY, after a busy week where she'd shared at least part of every shift with Nash, Kat knew quite the collection of new facts about him, admittedly none as thrilling or rebellious as his first admission. He'd once taken salsa classes, his party trick was juggling raw eggs and when he was seventeen he'd been a witness to a road accident, an event that had spurred his interest in medicine.

Only the most important thing she'd learned was that she hated her own rules with a vengeance. Kat was addicted, obsessed, convinced that the biggest mistake of her life was in fact insisting that their fling last only one night.

Apart from that single deviation, where he'd confessed that he wanted to kiss her again, Nash had frustratingly controlled his impulses, throwing Kat into a spin of conflicted emotions: one minute certain that friends was better, the next minute convinced his kiss was the only thing between her and insanity.

Leaving her latest patient and telling herself to get a grip and focus on her most pressing issue—that of childcare—Kat headed for the staff area in search of Nash.

She needed a favour and, to her surprise, he'd been her first choice of rescuer. Refusing to analyse at what point she'd progressed from thinking the worst of him to relying on him to help her out of a tricky school pick-up dilemma, Kat pulled her phone from her pocket and sent him a quick text.

Her heart thumped as she recognised just how much more she'd come to trust him since the night of his birthday when she'd trusted him with her body. But seeing his human struggles with solo parenting and hearing how he couldn't rely on his ex, how he'd been disregarded and betrayed, Kat felt more connected to him than ever, a state that was both exhausting and exhilarating.

While she awaited his reply, she typed up her observations on her current patient—a twenty-seven-year-old primip—a woman pregnant for the first time—with signs of pre-eclampsia. Henry had done such a good job of convincing Kat that there'd been something wrong with her for wanting Lucy she had to fight the urge to overanalyse if her plea for help was emotional dependence on Nash. But of course she wasn't reliant on him. They were friends and aside from her parents, who already did so much for Kat, it felt good to know she could ask him for help, that Nash would never let her down if it was in his power to assist.

As if sensing him nearby, the hairs on her arms prickled to attention.

'Yes, I can collect Lucy from school,' he said from right behind her, his voice low so no one else would hear. 'No problem at all.'

Instantly breathless, Kat spun around and smiled, her relief and gratitude all tangled up with lust. He was dressed in his own clothes, his blue shirt one of her favourites and his worn jeans moulded to his muscular legs and butt in all the right places. Oh, how she wished she could leave with him, suggest they take the girls to the beach for a stroll, watch them frolic in the waves, grab ice-creams and kiss on the sand...

Whoa, talk about taking a fantasy too far.

'Are you sure?' she asked. 'Because of course I'd planned to be out of here in time. This is a one-off request.' She'd do the same thing for him in a heartbeat, of course, but probably because Henry had criticised her choice, called her selfish, she was hesitant to rely too heavily on others.

He nodded, his eyes flicking over her face, settling briefly on her mouth. 'Positive.'

Kat exhaled a shaky breath, ignoring this lingering look the way she'd ignored all of the others this week. Even if he intended to make good on his admission and kiss her again, even if she was ready to turn their one night into a fling, there had been no opportunity. Their schedules were insane. One or other or both of them were either at work or after hours had commitments to their girls.

'Thanks, Nash.' His proximity was dangerous, as if the rest of the department, the patients and staff might disappear at any second. 'My… um…patient is twenty-six weeks pregnant and has pre-eclampsia. She needs to be admitted, but I won't be very long.' Even though her shift had ended fifteen minutes ago, medical staff often wanted to see a case through to admission.

His eyes softened, showing her that he understood that some cases were more personal than others, especially since she'd shared her own medical history with him.

'Kat, don't stress. You focus on your case, and I'll take the girls back to my house and give them a snack. You can swing by on your way home to pick Lucy up. Okay? Just call the school and explain.'

'I will. You are a lifesaver.'

In more ways than one.

Sometimes she couldn't shake the feeling that he'd brought her back to life, although the emotionally guarded and intimacy-starved woman he'd first met would have sworn there was nothing lacking in her life.

But to Kat, Nash's helpful gesture was a big deal. In the few weeks she'd known him, he'd shown Lucy more attention and kindness than her biological father ever had. Henry and Nash were as different as night and day. Nash praised her parenting, the compliment worth more coming from someone so dedicated to his own daughter, where Henry had seen her choice as selfish and reckless. His accusations wouldn't have carried half the weight if her pregnancy had been smoother, or if the timing of her father's debilitating stroke hadn't added to her guilt.

Forcing her thoughts back to her patient, she first called the on-call obstetrician to refer the woman and then the school, informing them that today Lucy was being collected by Nash. Such a momentous leap of faith gave her momentary jitters. She'd never thought she'd count on another man after Henry, but he was Lucy's father and she wouldn't trust him as far as she could throw him, let alone allow him to care for her precious girl.

The degree of faith she had in Nash was unprecedented, the comparisons between her worthless ex and the man showing her that some men could be relied upon feeding her growing feelings towards Nash.

Perhaps if she could trust him with her daughter she could trust herself to sleep with him again, to give her terrifying feelings a physical outlet, and trust him when he said that he wouldn't hurt her. Was she strong enough to share the kind of physical intimacy she knew him capable of and keep her heart out of harm's way?

An hour later as she drove to Nash's house from the hospital, her stomach flutters doubling with each passing minute, she tried to contain her excitement. Following the directions Nash had sent, she parked outside his neat weatherboard villa, her hands literally trembling. His front garden was well-maintained, and she spied a trampoline over the fence at the side of the house, the very thing Lucy wanted for Christmas. Kat would struggle to ignore her daughter's pleas now that Molly had the very thing Lucy coveted.

When Nash opened the door, his body language relaxed and his feet bare, Kat's mouth dried to ash. Why did she find his chill, everyday charm so sexy when it had been the first thing about him she'd also found annoying? But caring for the girls, reliable and trustworthy, and don't forget his skills between the sheets. Kat had to bite her lip to stop herself from dragging him close for a kiss right there and then.

'Hi,' she croaked feebly, her body practically melting into a puddle on his doorstep.

'Come in. They're on the trampoline,' he said, his easy yet somehow also knowing smile encouraging her pulse rate to triple.

'Of course they are.' She laughed in defeat. 'You do realise that I'll be tormented between now and December—a trampoline is the only thing on Lucy's Christmas list.'

'In that case,' he said, leading her through the house until they came to a sunny living area, 'we can let them enjoy it for a while longer. Would you like a drink?'

'Sure,' Kat said as they headed for the kitchen. 'Tea would be great.'

The sliding doors were open and Kat ducked out onto the deck to wave hello at Lucy and Molly. Her daughter, too busy bouncing, barely registered her mother's presence.

'There you go,' Nash said, placing a mug of tea on the bench in front of her, his gaze sliding up her body to her eyes in a slow and obvious perusal that left Kat doubting the wisdom of entering his home.

Their eyes met. All pretence seemed to slip away. All that remained were two people ridiculously attracted to one another who'd agreed to be just friends.

Giddy and breathless, Kat looked away first. 'Thanks,' she said, pulling out a bar stool and taking a perch. Even with their daughters a few metres away, when there was absolutely no chance of anything physical happening between them, he was tempting enough that she required the physical barrier of the kitchen island to stop herself from taking that kiss she hadn't been able to stop thinking about since he'd casually mentioned it.

She took a scalding sip of tea, desperate to do something, anything, with her mouth other than snog him or tell him about her fling idea.

'I'll give you fair warning,' Nash said, resting his forearms on the bench in a way that meant she could lean forward for that kiss, meet him halfway, 'they're planning to beg for a sleepover. I heard them plotting. Who knew five-year-olds could be so devious?'

'We did,' Kat said, laughing to hide her own request for a sleepover in Nash's bed. If only it was that simple...

'Lucy's never had a sleepover with a friend,' Kat said, trying to keep his eye contact instead of staring at the way his mouth moved.

'Neither has Molly. I think they're a bit too young, but they've clearly heard of the concept at school.'

'I agree. I'd worry that she'd change her mind in the middle of the night and wake you up.' Kat swallowed the lump in her throat, in awe of how wonderful a father Nash was.

Because Kat was close with her own father, she knew that Molly was a very lucky little girl. Poor Lucy would never know that kind of male role model bond.

'If you have tomorrow off,' Nash said, looking at her with that intense focus again, 'I wondered if you'd like to come with us to the aquarium. I promised I'd take Molly—she's obsessed with the penguins.'

Kat eyed him as he slowly stepped around the end of the kitchen island, her tea forgotten.

'That sounds good.' Her voice croaked. Her temperature soared at the thought of spending all day with Nash away from work, even with the girls as a barrier. Perhaps she could hurl herself into the water with the fish to cool down.

'Although…' she said, trying not to moan at the clean manly scent of him.

He frowned. 'Although…?'

Kat hesitated, her stare searching his. She was out of her comfort zone when it came to being open and vulnerable with a man she found so addictive. But Nash wouldn't judge her for her caution. He shared her reservations about bringing a new person into Molly's life.

'Do you think it might confuse them?' she said, longing gripping her throat while the old protective urges knotted her stomach. 'Us spending time together, I mean.'

She and Nash being friends along with their daughters was one thing, but they had to take care not to act like one big happy family.

She blinked away the vision, blocking out the dying excitement she saw in Nash's eyes.

She couldn't allow her libido to drive the bus unsupervised. Nash was a great guy, but relationships were tricky and time-consuming. That was why she had rules. Nash must have faults; everyone did. He was divorced, so obviously lacked something as a husband, even if he and his ex had been mutually responsible for the marital breakdown.

Kat glanced into the garden to stop herself from imagining Nash as a husband. The girls were still laughing on the trampoline.

'I think we're responsible parents, both wary of hurtful attachments,' he said, his voice calm and reassuring as he pulled out the stool next to hers. 'I understand your concerns, for Lucy and for yourself.' His expression brimmed full of compassion.

He saw through her thinly veiled attempt at keeping distance for her own sake too. If he could tell what she was thinking, did he also know how much she wanted him still?

She nodded, too turned-on and emotionally conflicted to speak.

'You're worried that if we spend too much time together Lucy might become attached to me, mistake me for a father figure?' Nash tilted his head in that way he had when he was listening to a patient. 'I have the same concerns for Molly. I've seen the way she relates to you.'

Kat felt see-through, as if she were made of glass. She certainly felt as fragile. This thing with Nash was dangerous. It reminded her how it felt to be emotionally vulnerable, to risk rejection, not just for herself but also for Lucy, who was old enough to grow attached to any man in Kat's life, but especially this man, as the wonderful father of her best friend.

They needed to tread so carefully.

'I'm probably being overprotective,' she said, trying to stave off stupid tears, because Lucy would be as lucky as Molly to have a father figure like Nash. Even the idea of it made her stomach twist. It was best not to think about such an impossible and risky scenario.

'If you are, I am too,' Nash said in his reasonable way. 'Look, if you think the aquarium is a good idea we'll just tell them the truth, that we're friends who work together.'

'Good idea.' Kat nodded, captive to the way he looked at her.

She should feel relieved that he was mature and responsible enough to consider her and Lucy's feelings as well as his own and Molly's. Instead, she wanted to selfishly hurl herself at him, to kiss him the way she had on her doorstep that night, regardless of the consequences. To remind him that friends didn't know how to pleasure each other's bodies to the point of exhaustion, didn't look at each other as if they were seconds from doing it all over again.

Only they had become friends, something she valued as much as him ending her sexual drought.

'Thanks for bailing me out today,' she said as he took a seat, his knee bumping her thigh.

'Stop thanking me. I'm certain you'll be able to repay the favour some time. It's no big deal.'

'It's a big deal for me.' Her voice emerged as a choked whisper.

Their eyes met. As if he knew her thoughts, as if he could read every one of her insecurities and doubts, Nash placed his hand on hers where it rested on the bench top. 'You don't have to do everything alone, Kat. Just because we chose to be parents, it's okay to ask for help. If I can be the one to help you, I will.'

She nodded, overcome by his touch, his thoughtfulness, his steadfast presence. She turned her hand over until their palms connected, fingers entwined, tiny jolts of electricity zapping along her nerves, his stare dancing between her eyes and her mouth. Her entire body shuddered.

Oh, please let him be about to kiss her...

'Are you ready for today's Nash fact?' he asked, his thumb tracing a lazy circle in the centre of her palm, flooding her blood with hormones so she was seconds away from ripping his shirt off.

She laughed, nodded, deaf to the sounds of their daughters playing in the garden. Immune to the fears and guilt that had held her back for six lonely years.

Desire this strong was too hard to fight.

He smiled, a slowly stretching upward curve of his tantalising lips that Kat watched with almost obsessive concentration.

As if he was thinking about how their kisses had tasted, he licked his lips. 'I like that you call me Nash when everyone else calls me Grady.'

'It's your name.' Kat's voice was the pathetic feeble whisper of a woman so turned-on that she might actually combust.

'It is, but it feels intimate when you say it. My favourite time was when I was inside you and you moaned it against my shoulder.'

'Nash…' Kat's eyes rolled closed. His words, his reminders, the feel of her hand in his—it was all too much.

She wanted him ten times more than she'd wanted him the night of his birthday. She deserved something casual and fun with a man she could trust in the bedroom but, like her, had no interest in commitment. As long as she was careful to keep her feelings out of it and hide it from Lucy, it was perfect.

He took her face in both of his hands. She opened her eyes.

'I can't stop wanting you,' he said, his stare locked with hers.

She nodded her agreement, too spellbound for speech.

'I know I'm breaking the rules.' His fingers tunnelled into her hair. 'If you want me to stop, I will.'

Her hands found his hips and she leaned closer. 'Kiss me.'

His lips grazed hers in a tease, one brush, two. Then he sealed their mouths together.

The breath stuttered out of Kat's lungs as she kissed him back, her fingers finding the belt loops of his jeans so she could pull him between her legs. He groaned as she parted her lips, his tongue sliding against hers, his hands tilting her head for better access.

Kat allowed desire to take her, the usual doubts silenced. All that remained was Nash, his kiss making her feel cherished and wanted and strong, his arms there to catch her if she slid from the stool, his passion the reward she'd craved since she'd watched him walk away the night they'd slept together.

He pulled back, breathing hard and looking down into her eyes with such intensity he almost looked angry or confused, but then he was kissing a path along her jaw and down her neck, his hand under her top caressing her breast.

Kat had a fleeting thought that she should stop, but instead she exposed her neck to his mouth, her own hands exploring the warm smooth skin of his back under his T-shirt. His muscles bunched and flexed under her palms and she recalled the way he'd scooped one strong arm around her and rolled them when they'd been naked and tangled in her sheets.

As if he was recalling the exact same memory, Nash's thumb worked over her nipple, coaxing the sensitive peak to harden as he watched her reaction through hooded eyes.

'Dad, there's a butterfly in the garden,' Molly yelled from outside.

Kat and Nash were dragged to their senses.

They sprang apart as a thunder of footsteps echoed across the wooden deck. By the time the girls came hurtling into the kitchen, Kat and Nash were once more on either side of the island, their clothes righted but their breaths still coming in pants.

Willing her frantic heart to settle, Kat stood and turned to face her daughter, praying like crazy that she didn't look as guilty and caught-out as Nash.

Lucy's excited chatter about monarch butterflies and the wonders of trampolining sharpened Kat's guilt for behaving so recklessly. What had she been thinking? How would she have explained that to Lucy if they'd been discovered necking and feeling each other up? Nash's *friends who work together* description certainly wouldn't have convinced her beady-eyed five-year-old.

'Can Lucy stay for a sleepover, Dad? Can she, please?' Molly drew out the last word for at least five seconds so show her commitment to pleading.

Kat shot Nash a grateful look, relieved to see humour and residual desire in his eyes. When it came to parenting, forewarned was definitely forearmed.

'Um…not tonight,' he said. 'But why don't

you invite Lucy to come to the aquarium tomorrow instead?'

Molly didn't bother to issue the invitation. The girls just squealed and bounced up and down, as if it was all settled.

'If that's okay with Lucy's mum, of course,' Nash said, looking at her in their private, grownup way.

Kat gave a shaky exhale, her mind stuck on playing mummies and daddies with him rather than on organising a play date.

Reaching for her bag, she clutched it to her chest. The last thing she needed was to spend the day with temptation personified under the watchful gaze of two impressionable young minds. But who knew when she and Nash would next have a weekend off together? Disappointing Lucy also meant disappointing herself.

'I think that sounds like fun,' she said, wondering how on earth she would keep her hands off Nash while imagining all the things they could do if they ever had another chance to be alone…

Nope, *fun* was the wrong word for that kind of torture.

CHAPTER TWELVE

GRADY POPPED THE boot of his car and reached inside for Lucy's backpack while Kat freed her daughter from her car seat. Waving a cheerful goodbye to Molly, Lucy ran ahead into the house. Kat placed the booster seat back into her own vehicle.

He'd argued that they had to virtually pass Kat's place to travel to the aquarium, but really he'd just wanted to spend the extra twenty minutes with her in his passenger seat so they could share secret glances and stolen smiles throughout the too short journey. He'd lost count of the number of times he'd almost reached for her hand while driving, and the number of times she'd grinned and winked as if she knew exactly what he was thinking.

Except she'd probably be shocked by how badly he wanted her still and how hard he'd fought to keep his hands off her all day.

Kat met him at the back of his car, taking Lucy's backpack, which she clutched to her chest like a shield. 'Thanks for a lovely day. Hopefully we've worn them out and we'll be able to bring forward bedtime tonight.'

Their eyes met, all kinds of grown-up communication passing between them, none of which could be voiced in front of their girls. He knew she wanted to touch him, saw it in the way she shifted her weight from foot to foot, her eyes darting to the back of the car every few seconds.

'You're welcome.' Grady smiled, his body wound tight like a spring because he too wanted nothing more than to haul her into his arms and kiss her goodbye. He wouldn't change a thing about today apart from this moment, wishing he and Kat could climb inside a bubble of invisibility for a few stolen seconds.

Not that it would be enough. He'd want Kat to come over once Molly was asleep, to share a glass of wine or a beer with her out on the deck, watching the sunset, to hear her dreams and her laughter and know that he was responsible for the beautiful smile on her face.

'Thanks for joining us,' he said, prolonging the moment.

'You're welcome,' she replied, playing along.

He stepped closer, checking that they weren't being observed over the top of the still-open boot. 'I wondered if you're free tomorrow,' he asked, subtly reaching out to tangle his fingers with hers at her hip. 'I want to take you on a date, just the two of us.'

Her pupils dilated. He tugged her hand, bringing her closer still, his reward a wave of her scent.

'Oh…what did you have in mind?' She looked up at him, playfulness and excitement in her eyes.

Being unable to touch her when he wanted, sneaking around behind their daughters' backs was torture. But he loved that he could put that relaxed and dreamy look on her face, that he could take away her wariness, that she'd seemed carefree all day in his company.

He shrugged in answer, his grin wide. 'Anywhere you like.' As long as they were alone, holding hands, free to touch while getting to know more and more about each other.

'We could see a movie,' he suggested, 'or take a walk on the beach. Coffee? Molly's spending the day with her grandparents so whatever works best for you.' He wanted to hog her to himself all day, but he understood the pressures of organising childcare.

She nodded, that now familiar longing in her eyes. 'Okay, I'll see what I can do. How about brunch?' Her stare dipped to his mouth.

He was going to have to kiss her, otherwise he'd regret it for the rest of the day and all of the night until he saw her again tomorrow.

'Sounds good.' Bolder now because Molly was engrossed in a book, his free hand settled on her hip so he could draw her lower body flush with his. 'I'll book somewhere.'

She licked her lips, distractingly beautiful, and slowly shook her head. 'Let me organise something.' She lowered the backpack and placed her other palm flat on his chest, over his galloping heart.

Kat glanced down the empty driveway for Lucy, but they were as alone as they could be.

'Great minds think alike,' he said, scooping his arms around her waist and hauling her up to his kiss.

The thud of the backpack hitting the driveway made him smile. Kat speared her fingers through his hair, her body languid in his arms. He caressed her mouth with his, their lips moulded together as if carved from the same piece of marble. He sighed, his breath mingling with hers as she parted her lips, their tongues touching, teasing, tangling, a goodbye kiss he hoped ended all goodbye kisses.

His groin tightened and he spared a fleeting thought for Kat's neighbours. If he didn't stop soon, they might get more of a show than he'd anticipated.

Why was it so hard to resist Kat Collins, and how could he slow down the train, because it felt as if there was grease on the tracks?

'You are so sexy,' he murmured against her lips. 'I couldn't tell you what the penguins looked like because I was watching you the whole day, wondering how long I'd have to wait to do this.'

He kissed her again, enjoying the feel of her hands gripping his biceps and her breasts crushed to his chest as she exhaled a soft whimper that made him almost forget that he had parental responsibilities.

But their daughters were the number one priority for each of them. That didn't mean he wasn't already looking forward to tomorrow.

She pulled away. 'Right,' she said, tugging down the hem of her T-shirt. 'Enough of that.'

A pink glow suffused her face and neck and she was breathing hard. Grady's feet were like concrete as he tried to catch his own breath. It was going to be so hard to walk away. But no matter how much they wanted each other, the girls came first.

'I'll see you tomorrow.' She retrieved the backpack and stepped back out of arm's reach, her expression stern, as if willing him not to follow. 'Brunch—it's a date.'

'Text me when and where and I'll be there.' Grady grinned, already keen to get home and fall asleep so he could wake up in the morning.

'I'll pick you up,' she said, laughing and backing up towards her front door.

The last thing he saw before she disappeared inside was her excited eyes and seductive smile, full of promise.

How was he so lucky to have met a woman like Kat? The more he got to know her, the more there was to like. She was warm and compassionate and had a great sense of humour. He could tell her anything.

He drove home, half his attention on Molly's chatter about penguins and Lucy and Kat and the other half on the woman who was now barely recognisable compared to the Kat he'd first met. She was so much more open than the prickly perfectionist of her first shift at Gulf Harbour. That she'd started to trust him, coming to him for advice at work and even asking for his help with Lucy, made him want to always be there for her, to never let her down.

He gripped the wheel, aware that he hadn't thought about the future in relation to a woman since Carol. Was he becoming serious about Kat and, if so, how would that even work?

They saw each other almost every day at work, spent a lot of time together at the hospital. Could they also have a personal relationship without taking each other for granted, allowing resentment to grow because they'd spent too much time in each other's company? He had enough grief from the upheaval Carol still caused. And he owed it to Molly to provide a stable home life.

'Dad, can we see Lucy and Kat tomorrow?' Molly said, dragging Grady from his ruminations. 'They can come to Nana and Granddad's house with me.'

Grady's stomach sank a little at the perfect timing of his daughter's request. Was Molly already becoming attached to Kat, as they feared? What if he made space in his life for a relationship with Kat and it didn't work out and Molly was hurt again? Kat's longest relationship had been with Lucy's father, before it turned sour, and he was a divorcee. Relationships ended. He wouldn't risk Molly being abandoned by another woman in her life because he'd rushed into something that wasn't right.

'Not tomorrow, gorgeous. Nana and Granddad want to have you all to themselves.' And, besides, he had his own plans for Kat, plans that he'd have to ensure included keeping things between them light and easy, proceeding with caution, controlling how much time Molly spent with Kat for as long as it lasted.

A hollowness settled in his gut. They'd barely started and he was already seeing their demise. Now he was the one being overprotective. Kat had been adamant that she wasn't interested in anything long-term.

He drove the rest of the way home, his buoyant mood dampened, and he couldn't for the life of him figure out why.

At eleven precisely the next morning Kat knocked at Nash's door, her stomach a riot of nervous anticipation. She was so worked-up she couldn't imagine eating one mouthful of the delicious brunch she'd prepared.

Just as well she had other plans for Nash.

After a minute or so he opened the door, his smile wide, his eyes sparking with the same excitement, making her hands tremble.

She swept her gaze over him, appreciation warming her blood. He was casually dressed for their date, the ends of his hair still damp from a shower.

'Hi,' he said, opening the door wider and inviting her inside.

'I brought brunch.' Kat presented the platter of bagels and various DIY toppings his way and stepped over the threshold, the idea of having him all to herself forcing her pulse so high she might actually pass out.

'Has Molly been picked up?' she asked as she followed him to the kitchen.

'Um…yeah, an hour ago. My parents are taking her for the day.' Nash looked confused as Kat took the platter from him, placed it in his fridge and slipped off her cardigan.

'Well, I only have a couple of hours,' she said, edging closer, slipping her hands around his waist, her intent obvious. 'My parents can only have Lucy for the morning.'

She tilted her face up to his, desperate to kiss him again after the torture she'd had to endure all day yesterday. 'Kiss me,' she said, looping her arms around his neck to bring his mouth down to cover hers.

He obliged with that sexy smile of his, catching on to her plan to skip the outing, backing her up against the kitchen bench so he could thoroughly ravage her mouth.

Kat moaned, loud and long. This kiss was the one she'd kept inside since that evening they'd been interrupted by the girls. Kat had fantasised about a different ending, her wild imagination spiralling out of control until she'd almost snogged him in the penguin enclosure.

Now, free from little prying eyes, her hands

roamed his taut body, the muscles of his back, his broad shoulders and corded arms.

She'd spent hours getting ready to see him today, lathering her body in her favourite body lotion after her shower, wearing the only sexy underwear she owned, dressing for him in the blouse he'd once complimented her on.

Kat slipped off her shoes and hopped up on his bench, tugging him between her spread legs. She pushed his T-shirt up, broke free for a second from his lips so she could raise the garment from over his head, but then their mouths connected once more and Kat collapsed forward into his arms.

She was so turned-on she'd probably agree to kitchen sex, uncaring if his neighbours had a bird's eye view. Aware of the seconds passing, Kat reached for the button of his jeans.

'Whoa…wait,' Nash said, clasping her wrists. 'I wanted to take you on a proper date.'

'I appreciate that, but time is precious.' And she didn't want to waste one second by leaving the house. 'Yesterday was torture, not being able to touch you, to do this.' Her hands tangled in his hair and she kissed a path down his neck.

'You don't play fair,' he groaned, his hands flexing on her hips. Then, with a grunt of defeat that made her heart sing, he scooped her up into his arms and strode towards his bedroom.

The rest of their clothes came off in record time, to Kat's utter relief. They stumbled onto the bed, collapsing in a tangle of arms and legs, moans and giggles until Nash ended up on top.

He looked down, pushed her hair back from her face with both hands and stared deep into her eyes, slowing the pace.

'You are so beautiful. I haven't been able to stop thinking about you, about this, since the night of my birthday. You're always in my head. All of the time.' He pressed a chaste kiss to her lips, cupping her face with such tenderness her vision blurred.

Nash was the whole package and she didn't want to think about how dangerous that made him. She didn't want to think at all.

'You're in my head too,' Kat whispered, her heart thumping against his warm wide chest. She pressed her lips together in case she said more—that she'd imagined them being a couple, eventually moving in together, those fantasies so tangible she'd had to shut them down and re-mind herself what had happened the last time she'd been invincible and reached for the stars.

To focus on the pleasure to be had in his arms alone, she spread her thighs, welcoming him into the cradle of her hips, crying out when he took one nipple inside his mouth, laving the peak with slow flicks of his tongue.

She could allow this physical indulgence, but more than that terrified her. How could they navigate a relationship when they could barely touch each other without serious implications? How would he and Molly fit into her already full life? Nash also had an ex-wife to deal with. There were so many variables. He'd been adamant that he wasn't looking for anything serious. She'd be a fool to ruin such a good thing with feelings.

'How are we going to do this again?' she asked in between gasps of delight as he teased first one breast and then the other. 'I already know that I'll want you tomorrow and the day after.' And she needed the next time to look forward to before this time was even over.

But Kat was an obsessive scheduler, the only way she could juggle everything successfully, so she knew for certain how precious and rare her free time was. It seemed impossible, the cruellest form of deprivation. They spent so much time together, but never alone.

'We'll figure something out,' Nash said, kissing a path back up to her mouth, his confidence and the intense look in his eyes appeasing her for now.

'Nash…' she pleaded, stroking her nails up and down his back because she'd learned that it made his hips flex as if involuntarily and his eyes darken with desire.

Was she imagining that she saw something more there? Was her own longing clouding her judgement, the way it had been way off before, with Henry? How could a grown woman be so wrong about a relationship? She was older and wiser now, knew what she wanted physically. But emotionally? She'd spent so many years shutting down those needs, focused instead on the needs of her daughter, that she still couldn't trust her feelings.

When Nash reached over to the night stand for a condom Kat almost fled, so deep was the emotional chasm at her feet. But then he was back on top of her, his strength surrounding her and his eyes communicating his wants and desires as he pushed his way inside her.

For the longest time he stilled, the only movement the matching beats of their hearts, chest-to-chest, stare-to-stare. Kat held her breath, her eyes swimming out of focus as she held him tight and tried her hardest to just be in the moment, that perfect moment.

But she'd always struggled to separate physical and emotional intimacy. That was why she'd waited so long before selecting a new sexual partner. She couldn't help the feelings she had for this man, who'd shown her that she was worthy of care and attention, who welcomed her daughter too, treating her the same as his own when they spent time together.

As if he saw her doubts and dreams in her eyes, Nash tilted his head, his intense stare softening.

'Kat…' He stroked her hair away from her face and brushed the softest whisper of a kiss on her lips. 'It's okay. We'll figure it out together.'

Kat nodded. She had no idea what *it* was. He could have still been talking about how to solve their privacy issue, to ring-fence some alone time for the intimate moments neither of them seemed able to resist. But Kat heard more than that. Right or wrong, she trusted this man, a decent man. He'd once told her he had no interest in hurting her and she believed him. Whatever the outcome of their relationship, she knew they had the same priority: their daughters. She would trust the rest to fate.

Dragging her mind back to pleasure, Nash moved inside her, finding a rhythm that left them both gasping, clinging to each other as if this might be the last time. The tempo built and built until the frenzy of their coupling reached fever-point and they climaxed together, their cries mingling.

After, Kat lay in his arms, her face pressed to the comfort of his heartbeat, where his chest hair tickled her cheek. His fingers traced long strokes down her arm and back as their breathing slowed and their sweat cooled.

'Are you okay?' he asked, pressing his lips to the top of her head.

She nodded, so many conflicting wants clamouring inside her that there didn't seem to be any space for air. Physically, she was more than okay, but meeting Nash, becoming his lover, it had shown the gaping holes in her life, holes she'd ignored and neglected for far too long.

How many moments of contentment had she missed out on over the years because she'd abandoned her search for this intimate closeness? Not that what she had with Nash was commonplace, of that she was certain.

'I'm just happy,' she said, holding Nash tighter, as if afraid to let him go. Because the type of connection they shared was rare. Something to be cherished, for as long as it lasted. Something to always remember. Something she was so lucky to have found.

'Me too.' His arms held her a little closer and Kat sighed, content for now, but still thinking of the dreams she'd had as an optimistic younger woman, dreams of finding a soul mate, getting married, having a family.

'How much time do you have?' he asked, rolling her on top of him so her hair fell around her face in a tumble.

Kat's gaze flicked to his alarm clock for the time, although she knew exactly how many more minutes she had him all to herself, as if the countdown ticked aloud in her head. 'An hour.'

He nodded, his stare unreadable. 'I start night shifts this week. Do you have a day off?'

Kat swallowed her sigh. 'Wednesday.' That felt like a year away.

'Want to meet for *brunch* after school drop-off?' he asked with that sexy smile that she'd travel miles to see. Already he was growing hard again between her legs. Would there ever be enough hours in the day to quench this craving for his touch, his kisses, the way he looked at her and made her feel as if she was the only woman in the world?

'Absolutely,' she said, leaning forward to brush her lips over his. 'But won't you need to sleep?'

The idea of him coming over while the girls were at school filled her stomach with flutters, but she didn't want to wear him out.

'I'd happily sacrifice sleep to be with you.' He stroked her hair back and brought her mouth down to his, his hips jerking up from the bed.

The second time was less frantic, but as Kat crested another climax she knew without a shadow of doubt that she was totally addicted to Nash Grady, and couldn't escape the alarming feeling that it was like trying to hold water in your bare hands.

CHAPTER THIRTEEN

THE PRINTER SPEWED out the prescription and Kat added her signature, her thoughts lost in a delicious daydream of Nash. Due to his stint of night shifts, she hadn't seen him at work or at school since the weekend when they'd stolen a few hours together, her brunch abandoned in the fridge while they'd gorged their fill of each other instead.

The days felt like years.

But tomorrow was Wednesday, her day off. Her stomach somersaulted in anticipation. They had another *brunch* date, if you could call spending as long as possible in bed before they had to collect Lucy and Molly from school a date.

Kat smiled to herself, already planning what she would wear under her jeans and T-shirt. If he was going to strip her, to marvel at her body as if he was unwrapping a gift, she wanted to wow him.

Something brushed her exposed neck, a soft almost incidental glide of fingertips under her hairline. She turned, her shock morphing into delight as she took in Nash standing behind her.

'What are you doing here?' she asked, glancing around the staff area to check that they were alone. They weren't doing anything wrong by seeing each other, but they hadn't discussed going public as an official couple and Kat liked that their relationship felt like a decadent secret only they knew.

'I just called in to resolve some work matters,' Nash said, his manner a little distant. 'Do you have a second?'

Dispirited that he seemed distracted, Kat nodded.

'Good. We can talk in my office.' His walk was businesslike. Kat followed him into the tiny room he only used when conducting a meeting or if he needed to reprimand one of the nursing staff.

Her pulse accelerated as he closed the door, her confusion turning to a shudder of relief when he pressed her up against the wood and kissed the living daylights out of her. Kat responded, kissing him back with pent-up desperation, her guilt at behaving inappropriately at work heavily outweighed by her constant need for Nash.

The old adage was true; absence did make the heart grow fonder or, in the case of Kat's heart, grow more and more terrified that she was becoming so dependent on him for her happiness that she'd started to see a future, hear wedding bells, imagine another baby with Nash's dark colouring and her big eyes.

Eventually and way too soon for Kat's liking, he pulled away, rested his forehead against hers while they both caught their breath.

'I missed you,' he said, his eyes closed, his heart still thundering under her palm.

He'd called into the department when he should be asleep, just to kiss her.

'I missed you too. I can't wait for tomorrow.' She swallowed hard, forcing down the feelings that were becoming impossible to ignore. But a few snatched minutes in their work environment wasn't the time or the place to ask him how he felt about her and confess that she wouldn't be averse to them having a proper relationship.

His phone pinged and he pulled it from his pocket, his face slashed in a harsh frown as he read the screen.

Kat's stomach swooped, anticipating the blow. 'What's wrong?'

For a minute he didn't answer, only straightened, moved away, muttering under his breath so she knew it was bad news.

'Is it serious?' she asked, imagining every possible scenario.

He shook his head. 'I don't know. I hope not.' When he looked up from his phone, his stare was bleak with worry. 'Carol,' was all he said. He rubbed a hand over his tired face.

Kat wanted to go to him, to hold him, but he still hadn't fully explained. 'Is Molly okay?'

He shook his head. 'She's fine. I just got Carol's invitation to mediation at family court. She wants to discuss changing our custody arrangement.'

Kat stifled a shocked gasp, appalled on his behalf. She touched his arm. 'That sounds scary.'

Nash pressed his lips together, distracted, perhaps deciding how much to share.

She looked away from the hesitation on his face, embarrassed for prying. They weren't a couple. His private life was none of her business. Just because her trust for him deepened day by day didn't mean that he owed her any explanation or loyalty. That the realisation stung told Kat just how emotionally invested she'd become in this man.

'I'm sorry. I need to go,' he said with a sigh. 'I need to speak to my lawyer.'

'Of course. Is there anything I can do to help?'

He must be worried. Molly was happy and

settled with their current custody arrangement. Surely there would have to be a very good reason to alter it. Nash was supportive of Carol's relationship with their daughter, but he wouldn't want to sacrifice any more of his time with his daughter.

He shook his head, his eyes filled with sadness. 'No. Thank you. I'm afraid I'll have to cancel our plans for tomorrow.'

Kat ducked her head, ashamed of her disappointment, which left her calculating how long they'd have to wait for another opportunity to be alone. 'Of course, no problem.'

The ache in her chest was evidence of her investment. She had no role in this situation, regardless of her feelings for Nash and Molly. Their daughter's welfare was between him and Carol. Kat wasn't even Nash's girlfriend, and if he wanted her there he would have asked.

Redundant and deflated, Kat focused on the big picture. Molly was his priority. That he was such a dedicated father was one of the things she loved about him.

She froze, the 'L' word buzzing in her head like a wasp. She didn't love Nash, did she? She couldn't. It was way too soon. Surely she was simply heavily in lust, cared about him as a person and valued his friendship.

That didn't make it love.

But would she even know? She'd thought that she'd loved Henry but that had felt totally different.

Easily dismissing her mini freak-out, she glanced back at Nash, who was collecting his bag from the ground. 'Hopefully her request will come to nothing, but I have to be seen to go through the motions of mediation.'

Kat nodded.

'I hate letting you down,' he said, pacing to his desk, obviously preoccupied.

She shrugged, desperate to feel as unaffected as she acted. 'Molly is more important. We can reschedule any time.' She meant it, but the words also left a bad taste in her mouth. Nash wasn't hers. Regardless of her feelings and fantasies, nothing had changed. Molly already occupied the place at the centre of his world and she wouldn't have it any other way.

He nodded, rearranging some papers on his desk. 'She does this, Carol. Flits in and out of Molly's life, causing maximum disruption. She's just messing with me.'

'Why would she do that?' Kat asked, genuinely puzzled. Just like Molly was the most important person in Nash's life, Lucy was the centre of Kat's. That was what happened when you became a parent; you put your child's welfare above your own.

Nash snorted. 'Because she can.'

She'd never seen him so bitter. Of course he felt threatened. Kat would fight to her dying breath to keep custody of Lucy. Clearly Nash had some serious issues to deal with. Their cancelled date was irrelevant.

'You should go, do what you have to and then try to get some sleep,' she said, ignoring her selfish yearnings, her jilted dreams.

'Thanks for being so understanding,' he said, stepping close once more.

Cupping her face, he brought their lips back together, this kiss tender and full of regret.

For a second Kat surrendered, trying to ignore the niggles of doubt taking root. Irrespective of how good it felt to be with him, irrespective of her wild imaginings of a shared future, they both had other responsibilities beyond their own needs and wishes. The part of her that had spent hours looking forward to their precious time together couldn't help but feel cheated. But it was a timely reminder that starting a new relationship was a pretty low priority for Nash. Kat needed to protect herself and, in doing so, protect Lucy. She didn't want to be the victim of a one-sided love affair again.

But when the kiss came to an end and she saw the tension in Nash's expression her concern for both him and Molly expanded. It was too late to pretend that she didn't care.

'I'll let you get back to work,' he said, effectively leaving Kat out in the cold.

He didn't want to share his feelings. He didn't need her right now.

Her pager vibrated in her pocket, telling her she was needed in Resus, a prompt that duty called. 'I need to go,' she said after reading the digital display. She swallowed the lump of hollow loneliness, the fear that she could no more rely on Nash to always be there for her than she could Henry.

When it came to the crunch she was still alone.

'Good luck for tomorrow.' She stuffed her hands in her pockets to stop herself from touching him again, dusting off the guard she'd mistakenly thought she no longer required. Experience had taught her how it felt to be second best, rejected, discarded. She had no desire to expose herself and Lucy to that kind of hurt once more.

'Thanks. I'll let you know the outcome,' Nash said, once more focused on his phone.

She opened the door and backed out of the room, stealing one last look at his worried face. Compassion squeezed her heart. How, in all her enthusiasm for what she'd found with him, had she missed the glaring reality that Nash had a lot to deal with and clearly wasn't in the right space for a new relationship? Pushing for more than the snatched scraps they had now would only lead to more heartache. She couldn't allow those crazy dreams of the future, her feelings and especially the scary 'L' word to take hold.

She just couldn't risk it.

CHAPTER FOURTEEN

THE NEXT DAY Grady pressed Kat's doorbell, the need to see her so strong he was worried he might rip the door from its hinges with impatience. He exhaled, trying to find calm after his incredibly frustrating morning. The meeting with Carol and the lawyers had been the typical waste of time he'd expected.

The door opened and Grady sagged with relief. The sight of Kat was like a ray of sunshine on a cold spring morning, raising his spirits and clearing his mind of all the extraneous chatter.

'Can I come in?' he asked, because Kat was smiling as if pleased to see him but also shocked.

'Of course.' She reached for his hand and drew him inside.

Acting purely on instinct, he pulled her into his arms, held her close, just breathed. The warmth of her body comforted him like a blanket, her scent now so familiar he loved that it clung to his shirt long after they'd spent time together. For a few seconds, with the thud of his heart slowing against hers, nothing else mattered.

'Are you okay?' she whispered finally.

He nodded, pulled back, his lips seeking hers in a kiss that was soft and desperate, his emotions spilling over, jumbled and startling in their intensity. She had no idea what she meant to him. How much he craved her or how a simple smile, a touch, a glance from her soothed his soul.

Breaking the connection of their lips at last, he rested his forehead against hers. 'I'm sorry. I just really needed to do that. I really needed you.' All of the tension of the day, his fears that he'd lose Molly, shuddered out of him as she smiled, pressed her lips to his once more, her hands stroking up and down his arms.

'Come in,' she said when she pulled back. She took his hand and led him into the lounge.

They sat on the sofa together, hand in hand. Grady wanted to pull her into his arms, to selfishly hold her for ever until all was right in the world. He swallowed, panic that his need for Kat had become so violent gripping his throat. When had that happened? How had she burrowed so deeply into his soul that she was his first thought when he opened his eyes in the morning, the person he wanted to share all of his daily trials and tribulations with?

Not that Kat needed his dramas. Her life was full with work, Lucy, her parents.

'What happened?' she asked, squeezing his fingers.

'Nothing major, just a lot of talk.'

'So nothing's changed for you and Molly?'

He shook his head. That she cared about him, cared about Molly, left him speechless. He'd spent the day wishing she was at his side, her calming presence and reassuring smile making sense of the crazy in his life.

Kat exhaled, her relief for him palpable.

Emotion compressed his lungs. He was falling for this wonderful woman in a way he couldn't be certain he'd ever fallen for anyone before. It reminded him of the terror of his very first parachute jump.

'I don't want to download my drama onto you.' He gripped her hand tighter, his frustration with Carol and worry for Molly already eased after a few minutes in her company.

In the same way they worked as an efficient and effective team at the hospital, Grady had the sense that together they could conquer any obstacle. But that was wishful thinking. He'd let Kat down today. He couldn't bombard her with his emotions, especially when he was too scared to tease them out for closer examination.

What if she didn't feel the same way about him?

'I don't mind listening,' she said softly, her gaze full of concern.

Grady sighed. His personal life was a mess and all he really wanted to do was hold Kat, lose himself in their passion, forget about the emotional wringer his ex continued to put him through.

'Carol likes to play games,' he said, wincing at the idea that his ex could potentially ruin what he had with Kat as she had interrupted their date today. 'She claims that she wants more time with Molly, which is crazy. She hardly ever uses the days she's supposed to take Molly. She just comes and goes as she pleases, regardless of what's best for Molly and usually when it's most inconvenient for me, like today.'

Kat nodded, her gaze flitting away. 'Does Carol know about me...about us?'

Grady froze, noticing Kat's distraction for the first time. 'I haven't told her.' His love life was none of Carol's business. The only access she had to his life was when it concerned their daughter. 'But she's been fishing, questioning Molly.' Sensing something about Grady had changed, Carol had figured out there was a new woman in his life. 'I think today was about making me jump through her hoops.'

'Why would she waste everyone's time like that?' Kat asked, frowning.

'Because she's upset that she can't call the shots with me any longer. She grabbed me after the mediation, said she wanted to talk about getting back together.'

Kat stiffened, her tension transmitted to him through their hands.

'She's done that before. Several times. My answer is always the same: no.' He understood Carol's desperation. Kat was the closest Grady had come to a relationship since their divorce. She could clearly sense the depth of his feelings for Kat and wanted to let him know that as Molly's mother she was still part of the picture.

Feeling as if Kat was slipping away, as if she didn't believe his assurances, he touched her chin, tilted her face up so their eyes met. 'I'm sorry that I let you down today. I promise that I'll make it up to you.'

'I was just a little disappointed, that's all.' She looked down, but not before he witnessed the doubt and uncertainty in her eyes. 'I don't want to make things difficult for you, Nash,' she said. 'It's understandable that Carol wouldn't want a random woman interacting with her daughter. I'd feel the same.'

'You're not some random woman, Kat.' He scrubbed a hand through his hair in frustration. 'I don't care how Carol feels about my private life.'

His ex never told him about the men she saw. Of course he would have told Carol about Kat eventually, but he'd wanted Kat to feel comfortable with him and Molly before he exposed her to his ex. His circumstances would put many women off, and he wasn't even sure if Kat had changed her mind about taking their relationship forward.

Perhaps she wasn't ready. Casual and fun was one thing. It was a whole lot more serious to take on not only him and Molly but a meddling ex-wife too. Maybe he was rushing it. He'd made that mistake once before. Perhaps Kat just needed more time.

'Okay,' she said, looking unconvinced, making him question her feelings. 'But we always said we'd put the girls first, so if you need for us to cool things down, that's fine.'

It might be fine with her but it rankled him that, through their daughter, his ex was still trying to exert some sort of hold over his life.

'Our joint responsibility for Molly doesn't give Carol any rights over my life, Kat.' Frustration twisted in his belly. Yes, his daughter came first, but that didn't mean he'd given up on his own search for happiness. He'd realised that yesterday when he'd received Carol's message, wishing that Kat was a serious part of his life so he wouldn't have to choose between his responsibilities and being with her. She'd be a part of his life, all areas of his life.

A trickle of apprehension snaked down his spine. Unless that idea filled her with horror.

He cupped her cheek, lured her eyes back to his. 'Is that what you want? For this to be over?'

Perhaps, for Kat, him and his complications were a risk not worth taking. His stomach churned. But he'd rather know now, before she became any more indispensable for his happiness.

'Of course not.' Sparks danced in the depths of her irises.

Grady exhaled, relief shunting his heart back into a steady rhythm.

'But Molly is the most important thing in your world, just as Lucy is in mine,' Kat continued. 'If our…fling is putting her happiness and yours at risk then…'

He gripped her face. He didn't want to hear how that sentence ended. He didn't want this to be over. He pressed his lips to hers, willing things to be the way they'd been at the weekend when, for him, it had moved beyond a fling.

'We haven't talked since we broke all of the rules...' he hedged, needing to know if she saw any future for them.

'No.' Kat's eyes widened, like a deer trapped in the headlights, forcing his pulse dangerously high. 'I guess that's what I'm trying to say. I want you, but I understand that you have other priorities.'

Grady nodded, his stomach plummeting. She wanted *him*. But what about Molly?

Was it still just about their physical connection for her? Even if she wanted a relationship, would she tolerate Carol trying to pull his strings, robbing them of their precious time, the way she had today?

Perhaps they should do the responsible thing, call things off before anyone's feelings became hurt. Except he was already way too invested to emerge from this unscathed.

Accepting defeat for now, he nodded. 'You're right. I do have other priorities, and I always will. That doesn't mean that I don't want you too.'

He winced at his hypocrisy and selfishness. Kat deserved more than a fraction of his attention. After the rejection she'd been through in the past, she deserved to be adored unreservedly. If he let her go, she could find someone without his baggage.

With impeccable timing, a text alert sounded on his phone. It was Carol, informing him she'd decided to collect Molly from school.

He sighed. 'I need to go. Carol has just turned up at the school.'

Kat nodded, standing. 'My parents are collecting Lucy today.' She walked him to the door.

Grady hesitated. Nothing was resolved.

The urge to pour out his feelings and beg her to keep giving them a chance gripped him as if by the throat. Maybe, with time, if they managed to carve out some space to allow their relationship to blossom, she'd come to feel the same way.

'Do you want to know today's revelation?' he asked, aware that he was rushing off and had no right to ask any more of Kat.

'Sure,' she said, her smile tinged with sadness, as if there was nothing he could tell her that mattered more than what they'd already said.

He prayed that wasn't true. That she'd learn to trust him enough to give another relationship a chance.

'I think you are a terrific mother, Kat,' he said. 'Lucy is a very lucky little girl to have you.'

Her eyes grew glassy, her stare raking his. 'I'm lucky to have her too, just like Molly is lucky to have you.' She took his hand, squeezed his fingers. 'You always put her first, Nash, and I wouldn't want it any other way.'

Of course she wouldn't, because she was wonderful and she'd been badly treated, had watched her lovely Lucy be badly treated.

He pressed a kiss to her cheek, walking away on heavy feet.

They shared the same dedication to their daughters. They shared a career and a sense of humour and incredible intimacy. The question was: would that be enough?

CHAPTER FIFTEEN

IT WAS UNUSUAL for the night shift to be quiet. In Kat's experience, night-time in the ER was often just as busy as the daytime, and she preferred it that way. Keeping busy left no time for thoughts, and in her current conflicted state there was only one topic on her mind: Nash.

She was no longer in any doubt that she'd fallen in love with him. His text was the first thing she looked for when she opened her eyes in the morning, their late-night phone call the last thing she wanted to do before she fell asleep, where, invariably, he filled her dreams.

And if she needed any more proof, her reaction when he'd told her that his ex had suggested they get back together, the seething hot jealousy, the nausea, had been the icing on the cake.

But just because she fallen didn't mean that their situation wasn't complicated. Perhaps sometimes love wasn't enough.

Kat's admiration for Nash and the way he

handled the various expectations placed on him in a calm, reasonable, considerate way was unwavering. If she had her choice of any man in the world she'd want a partner with whom she could weather any storm. A mature and compassionate man who put others first, even when it was hard and took personal sacrifice.

So why was she terrified of the many factors that might derail them from being more than friends and lovers?

Not that Nash had asked for more.

For a brief second, when he'd mentioned how badly they'd broken her rules, her heart had surged with hope. But every time she tried to picture the future that had been crystal-clear for a fleeting second, all she saw were barriers: Carol, the girls, even time seemed to be against them. It seemed impossible.

She couldn't fight the feeling that she was being selfish by bringing a man into Lucy's life, that it might fail and hurt them all—Kat, Lucy, Nash and Molly.

Frustrated that she'd spent the last ten minutes trying to see a way forward when she should have been revising for her trauma exams, Kat turned the page on her textbook and began reading the same paragraph on spinal immobilisation for the third time.

A sudden commotion, raised voices, had her

rushing towards the reception area and patient waiting room. Before she could get there the double doors swung open and Nash backed into the ER carrying Molly in his arms. She was dressed in her pyjamas and seemed to be struggling for breath.

'She's having an attack,' he said, his voice more urgent than Kat had ever heard.

Kat's heart lodged in her throat, panic pounding adrenaline through her blood.

'Tell me when it started.' Kat rushed after him as he strode into a nearby bay. She would need to set aside what the little girl meant to her and focus on her training. She couldn't allow the emotions she felt for Nash and his daughter to cloud her clinical judgement.

Nash placed a limp and docile Molly onto the bed, reaching for an oxygen mask, uncaring that he wasn't on duty and technically his role was that of a family member. 'She's got a cold at the moment, but I hoped we'd get away with it.'

Kat could hear Molly's pronounced wheeze from her position at the side of the bed.

'She's been coughing all night,' Nash continued, the distress in his voice urging Kat to comfort him. But Molly needed her more.

'Her oxygen sats dropped half an hour ago,' he said in full-on nurse mode. 'I have a monitor at home.' He tenderly placed the mask over Molly's face and turned on the flow of oxygen.

Kat understood his automatic actions; he was doing what needed to be done, as always. If it were Lucy lying there, she'd do the same. But he was also a parent and he needed to let Kat do her job.

Kat turned to the nurse on duty.

'Get me nebulised salbutamol and prednisolone, please.' Her gaze flicked to the digital monitor, which showed Molly's oxygen saturation to be an alarming ninety-one percent.

'I need to have a quick listen, Molly.' Kat kept her voice calm, even though her stomach knotted with worry. She loved this man. She loved his little girl, but she needed to be strong for them both, to keep her own panic well concealed. Showing Molly her distress would only make things worse.

She took her stethoscope from around her neck. 'It won't hurt, just might be a little bit cold.'

Nash unbuttoned Molly's pyjama top and Kat pressed the bell of her stethoscope over Molly's chest on each side, noting that the little girl was using her accessory muscles of respiration, a sign that the asthma attack was severe. Molly was working very hard to make her lungs function. She stared over at Nash while she listened to the lung fields, trying to show him with her eyes that she was there for him and Molly, that she'd do everything in her power to help. The helplessness in his eyes was hard to witness, but Nash knew the implications of a severe asthma attack as well as Kat.

Medical staff often treated the emotional needs of the entire family when a loved one was sick. Only Kat had never been so heavily invested. It was as if it were Lucy lying there struggling to breathe.

'No pneumothorax,' she said, looping her stethoscope back around her neck.

'Don't worry, sweetheart.' She smiled, took Molly's small hand and felt her feeble grip. The last thing she wanted to do was transmit any of her concern to Molly. 'We're going to make you feel all better, okay? I'm glad Daddy brought you in to see me tonight.'

The nurse returned with the medications and set up the nebuliser in place of the oxygen mask alone over Molly's mouth and nose. Kat and Nash stood on opposite sides of the bed, each holding Molly's hand. Her chest ached for him. Each time he looked at her his stare implored Kat to do something—anything. But he knew she was doing everything she could.

'Give me the rest of Molly's history,' Kat said while they waited for the drugs to work.

Nash answered Kat's enquiries about Molly's general health, the frequency of her asthma attacks and her regular medications. Kat fought the urge to reach out across the bed and take his free hand so they formed a tight little circle of comfort, but not only was she conscious of crossing professional boundaries, she also needed the physical distance to give her enough emotional distance that she remained objective.

More than ever, she needed to protect herself too. She wasn't Molly's mother. She and Nash were still technically casual. Any possible future for them would be complicated. He'd stated that he didn't want to get back together with Carol, but Kat couldn't help the insecurities that made her doubt his word.

Shoving her fears aside, Kat watched Molly breathe in the drugs, which formed an aerosolised mist in the mask. Each of Molly's inhalations and laboured exhalations added to the panic she was trying to keep at bay. The seconds seemed endless as she kept one eye on Molly and the other on the monitors, observing her respiratory rate and oxygen saturations, willing the numbers to move in the right direction. Willing Molly to recover.

Finally, the oxygen saturation reading improved to ninety four percent. Kat breathed a shaky sigh of relief, her stare taking in Nash's haggard features.

He looked to her, a glimmer of hope in his eyes.

Kat nodded, almost overcome by her love for both of them. It was a good sign that Molly might be out of danger.

Nash visibly crumpled a little. He silently mouthed the words *thank you*, his gratitude, his vulnerability, his trust, almost buckling Kat's knees.

Because her emotions were so close to the surface Kat feared he'd see them on her face, she looked down, blinking away the sting of tears. If only she could hold him, confess her feelings aloud, tell him that she loved both him and Molly and that together they'd make everything okay.

When had Nash and his daughter snuck under her guard and wormed their way so deeply into her heart? If she'd thought she loved him before tonight, she was even more certain now, his happiness and Molly's vital to her own.

Deciding that she owed it to herself to tell him her feelings, to ask him to give their relationship a chance, she would wait until Molly was out of danger and then find the right moment.

The curtains around the bed swished open and a woman rushed in. She was tall and slender, her blonde hair cut short in a sophisticated style, which looked good even though she'd clearly rushed there in the middle of the night.

Kat's stomach churned with nausea. This must be Carol.

'Darling, Mummy's here,' she said to Molly, standing at Nash's side, so close that their shoulders touched. Obviously concerned, Carol looked to Nash for an explanation.

'She's doing really well,' he said to his ex, his eyes flicking to Kat and then back to Molly.

Kat swallowed down the hot ball of tangled emotions in her throat.

Her envy was pointless. Nash and Carol had made a baby together, loved each other enough to get married. Of course he'd informed Molly's mother that he was taking her to the ER. They were co-parenting. In an emergency they were still a family. United.

Nash would always do the right thing and she loved his integrity.

So why did it feel like rejection?

Returning her attention to Molly, Carol placed her hand over Nash's so that they were both holding their daughter's hand.

'I'm her mother,' Carol said, her eyes darting between Nash and Kat as if she'd noticed the look they'd shared. 'Is she going to be okay?'

Kat was still holding Molly's other hand. The

other woman noticed this, her lips pursing with disapproval.

'I'm Dr Collins, one of the ER doctors,' Kat said, introducing herself to Nash's ex, the woman from whom Molly had clearly inherited her heart-shaped face. Kat refused to release Molly's hand. The little girl's previously feeble grip was growing stronger, a good barometer of her recovery.

'We're treating Molly with some nebulised medication and oxygen,' she explained, her voice reassuring. 'And it seems to be working.' Kat smiled at Molly, aware that being unable to breathe must be terrifying.

Carol spoke to Nash in a hushed voice, asking him for more details of the attack.

Excluded, Kat's isolation flared anew. She was an outsider. She wasn't part of Molly's family. Even if she and Nash committed to building a relationship, Carol wouldn't want to share her daughter with Kat, as she'd already proved with her request for more custody. No matter how deep Kat's feelings were, any relationship would struggle under the pressure of such enormous potential for conflict.

She looked away, tried to give them some privacy, busied herself by checking the monitors, re-examining Molly's chest.

'How are you feeling now, sweetheart?' She smiled down at Molly, the term of endearment just slipping out because she'd used it so many times before when Molly and Lucy were together.

'Where's Lucy?' Molly asked, speaking for the first time since she'd arrived in her father's arms.

Kat smiled, breathing easy for the first time. 'Lucy is at home asleep. But if you're feeling better, and if it's okay with Mum and Dad, maybe she can come visit you.'

She glanced at Nash, her relieved smile matching his. Her promise was probably unwise given the complexity of their situation. But Kat didn't have the heart to disappoint Molly, not after what she'd been through.

'Who's Lucy?' Carol asked, scrutinising Kat.

'My best friend,' Molly replied.

Reluctantly releasing Molly's hand, Kat moved to the work station and logged on to the computer. She ordered a chest X-ray for Molly and made some notes. She tried to give the family some privacy, but it was hard not to notice that while Carol comforted Molly, Nash remained quiet.

'I'm going to speak to the paediatric team,' Kat said, addressing Nash and Carol. 'We might just keep Molly in tonight for observation.'

They both nodded, their focus returning to their girl.

She left them alone, her heart heavy. It wasn't her place to explain her role in Nash's life to his ex-wife. Perhaps he'd never had any intention of telling Carol about Kat because his feelings for her weren't serious.

As she spoke to the on-call paediatrician her loneliness intensified.

Carol might not always be around, but she was still Molly's mother. Kat was happy that Lucy's friend had two parents to love her. She was even grateful that Nash could share the worries of parenting with someone. She knew how hard it was doing it alone.

But where did that leave her and Lucy?

A serious relationship with Kat would mean he'd also need to make room for Lucy. Would he consider it worth the effort, when his life was already complicated enough?

Returning to Molly's bay, she was about to open the curtains, to tell the family that Molly would soon be transferred upstairs to Paediatrics, when she heard the hushed and urgent voices of Nash and Carol.

She froze, aware that she shouldn't listen but desperate to make sense of tonight, her feelings, the implications of it all for her and Nash.

'I'm sorry I didn't answer as soon as you first

called,' Carol said. 'I'd gone out for a drink with the crew after work. That doesn't mean I don't care.'

'I know you care about Molly,' Nash said, his voice flat. 'I'm just tired of picking up the pieces after you let her down.'

Kat ached for him, for the toll tonight had taken.

'Well, if you would just listen... If we were a family again we'd all be under one roof, so you wouldn't need to call me.'

Kat shuddered, placed her hand over her mouth, Carol's plea for a reconciliation making her stomach churn with nausea. She should leave. She was invading their privacy. But her feet wouldn't move. Would Nash agree?

'You should think about Molly,' Carol continued, 'about what she wants.'

Part of Kat agreed with Carol's logic. After all, a complete family was what she'd wanted for Lucy. But a child wasn't enough glue to hold two people together and it was selfish to even place them in that position.

'You and I are a separate issue,' Nash said. 'I've told you before. I've moved on. Molly is all the family I need. I don't want to discuss this again.'

Kat heard the scrape of a chair on the floor,

her heart jumping into her throat. She scurried away before she was discovered eavesdropping.

It took her a solid five minutes to calm down, to perfect a convincing enough mask to face them again.

Chilled to the bone by her realisations and by what she'd overheard, Kat had never felt more alone. Despite the rules she'd put in place to protect herself, she'd not only fallen in love, she'd started to make future plans that involved Nash and Molly, as if they were already a blended family, before knowing Nash's feelings.

But Nash didn't want the same things. He was content as he was, just him and Molly. Kat was more vulnerable now than when she'd boarded a plane back to New Zealand, pregnant and heartbroken. Because she hadn't loved Henry as deeply as she loved Nash. Nash was the real deal, everything any woman would be lucky to have in a partner.

Only she was still very much alone, and loving him might turn out to be her biggest mistake ever.

CHAPTER SIXTEEN

LATER THAT MORNING Grady strode into the ER in search of Kat. Emotionally drained, his adrenaline spiked so high his hands trembled, every cell in his body clamoured for one glimpse of her before she went home after her night shift.

Last night had been one of the longest of his life, Molly's attack the worst one yet. He'd almost collapsed with relief the minute he'd seen Kat, the panic coursing through his veins easing. When she'd gripped Molly's hand, her reassuring gaze locking with his, he'd known in an instant that his feelings were undeniable.

He loved her.

Glancing around the department, he tried to slow his breathing, the sense of panic returning, as if Kat was slipping through his fingers like sand.

The timing of his eureka moment couldn't have been any worse. There'd been no time to talk to Kat, no time to touch her, no time for anything but using every scrap of his energy to will Molly well.

Spying Kat at last, he tried to get his emotions under control. She was talking to one of the male orthopaedic registrars, her smile wide and easy, the tinkle of her laughter causing Grady's skin to prickle hot with jealousy.

His muscles tensed in frustration. Kat deserved a straightforward relationship, one that put that carefree look on her face every day.

But what did he have to offer? A few snatched kisses and the mess of his complex personal life.

He dragged in a steadying breath. The emergency with Molly had rattled him to his bones. He needed a shower, a good night's sleep, some food. Until his daughter was home, no longer an inpatient on the paediatric ward, he'd need to shelve the urge to approach Kat and confess his feelings.

As if she sensed him behind her, Kat turned. Their stares locked, silent communication passing between them the way it did when they worked on the same case, when they smiled over something cute one of the girls said, when they were intimate.

But could that connection translate into a committed relationship? He knew how much work that took. Would Kat want to take that risk for him when he was currently able to give her so little in return?

Ending her conversation, she came to him, a small frown of concern on her face.

'How is she doing?' she asked, her compassionate gaze a balm for his weary soul.

Disappointed that she'd put her hands in the pockets of her lab coat, Grady fought the urge to drag her into his arms, to know she was his, that they'd work out the rest together. He didn't care if the whole department knew that they were more than friends and colleagues.

'Better. Thanks to you,' he said, trying not to sigh at the respectable distance she kept. Clearly she did care.

Gratitude swelled up inside him, threatening to block his throat. No matter what happened between him and Kat in the future, he'd always be indebted to her for helping Molly.

Kat shook her head, dismissing his compliment. 'You look exhausted. Do you want to grab a coffee from the canteen? I've just finished my shift and was about to head home so I'm free if you need to talk.'

She was so strong and kind and smart, and he loved her so deeply. He'd probably loved her from the minute she'd fixed that troublesome tiara.

He shook his head, regret like a stone in the pit of his stomach. 'I can't be away for too long.'

He did need to talk, to tell her he loved her, but it would have to wait. 'I've left Molly with Carol.'

The minute Molly was out of danger, thanks to Kat, he'd realised that he'd been holding himself back, scared to confess his feelings, scared he'd fail to be what Kat needed, scared he'd be rejected. Because more people than just he and Kat would be hurt if it didn't work out. Molly had been too young to remember Carol leaving. But as he'd watched Kat and Molly's connection last night he'd realised that his little girl was truly attached to Kat, a fact that hadn't escaped Carol's notice.

'Can you come to my office for a second?' Unease at Kat's continued distance gripped him. Had she planned to leave without checking on them? Something was definitely off with her, aside from her concern for Molly.

'Of course,' she said, ducking her head.

He strode to his office with Kat in tow. If he could get her alone, speak with her in private, he'd not only have some sense of how she felt about him, he could also ask her to give him some time to get things sorted.

Once inside, he shut the door, his heart pulsing in his throat with all that he wanted to say but needed to postpone.

Because he couldn't stand the distance, he took both of her hands in his. 'I'm so grateful to you, Kat. I know it happens every day around here, but you saved Molly's life. I can't tell you what that means to me.'

Kat nodded, blinked as if heading off tears. 'I know what she means to you,' she whispered and then cleared her throat as if brushing off the emotion. 'I was only doing my job.'

She sounded so reserved. He hadn't slept for thirty-six hours, but it wasn't just his imagination.

'I know it's your job—' he frowned '—but when you're on this side, as a worried parent…' Words failed him. They seemed to be making everything worse anyway. She looked even more withdrawn.

'You don't have to thank me.' She looked down at her feet. 'I'm sorry if Molly asking for Lucy created an issue for you with Carol.'

'Is that what's wrong? You're worried about Carol because she put two and two together about us?'

Of course his ex had volleyed a string of personal questions his way the minute Molly had fallen asleep. She'd noticed the bond between Kat and their daughter, witnessed the way he'd looked at Kat, not that his love life was any of Carol's business. She'd even used his vulnerability to push her agenda that they get back together again.

Kat winced, extricated her hands from his grip. 'She's Molly's mother, Nash. She always will be. She has every right to ask questions about the people in her daughter's life. I'd do the same.'

'I agree,' he said, feeling as if he was losing control of his train of thought. 'And I answered her questions, explained that Lucy is your daughter.' But that was where his loyalty to Carol ended. Until he and Kat had discussed moving their relationship from casual to serious, until he asked her to make them official, told her of his feelings, he had no obligation to inform Carol. And right now, exhausted, worried and confused by Kat's apparent withdrawal, his sense of where he stood with her was rapidly disappearing.

In that moment his phone rang. Seeing that it was Carol, he answered, speaking to her for a few seconds to confirm he was heading back to the ward as soon as possible.

'I'm sorry, I have to go,' he said to Kat after he'd hung up. 'The team are there for a ward round.' He needed to focus all of his energy on Molly's recovery so he could take her home, invite Kat and Lucy over to cheer her up, smother her with love and care until there was space in his head for his own needs. 'They are talking about discharging Molly later today.'

Kat stepped back. 'Of course. You should go.' She opened the door to his office and loitered on the threshold as if she couldn't wait to get away.

Part of him couldn't blame her. He had no idea if she wanted more, but he currently had nothing to offer her anyway, beyond vague promises. He wouldn't risk letting her down. Better to wait until they could talk it all through.

'I'm going to take the rest of the week off,' he said, hoping that they would find an opportunity to discuss their relationship. 'Obviously Molly and I will have to cancel the plans we made with you and Lucy for tomorrow.' They'd organised to share a barbecue at his house after school. Now he just wanted to take Molly home and wrap her up in cotton wool until she was once more her usual energetic self.

'I'd offer to help,' Kat said, looking down, avoiding his stare, 'but you and Carol will have everything covered, I'm sure.'

Nash opened his mouth to protest and then closed it again. He wanted to reassure her that for him, personally, he'd rather have Kat's help than Carol's. But it wasn't about *him*. It was about Molly, and Carol was her mother. If Molly wanted Carol around then that was what she'd have if it was in his power.

'I should go home, get some sleep,' she said, inching further away.

Unable to hold her, kiss her, reassure her, Grady curled his fingers into fists, wishing he could ask Kat to stay with him on the ward, but she'd been up all night too. Night shifts messed with your circadian rhythm. He should let her go, but he couldn't help the sickening feeling that this felt like a goodbye.

'Wait.' He scrubbed his hand through his hair, dread making him desperate to make things between him and Kat right. 'I know my timing is off, because I really do have to go, but I've been thinking about us for a while now—'

'It's okay, Nash,' she interrupted, holding up her hand to ward off his words. 'You don't have to explain. We always said it was temporary.'

She shoved her hands in the pockets of her white coat, her guard up. He was reminded of that prickly, rule-loving version of Kat that he'd encountered on her first day at Gulf Harbour. He'd assumed they'd moved past all of their differences, but maybe not.

He tried to think, his fatigued brain sluggish. 'I'm not calling it off if that's what you're thinking.' The idea spiked his adrenaline, panic leaving a metallic taste in his mouth.

He'd been about to tell Kat that he had feelings for her, that he wanted them to be an item, that they could take things at her pace, take it slow for the sake of their girls, but he wanted a proper relationship, not just the fling they'd squeezed in between work and their family commitments.

But she was already halfway out of the door, literally and figuratively had already begun shutting down from him and what they'd shared, reverting to the immovable Kat.

Had he totally misjudged her feelings for him and Molly? It wouldn't be the first time he'd rushed into a relationship.

Kat shook her head, looking like a cornered animal. 'It's okay if you are ending things. It's probably for the best. You have a lot going on, Nash—Molly, Carol—and the last thing I want—*or need*—is to get in the way.'

He stepped closer, willing her to hear him and not just run scared because she'd been hurt in the past. 'You're not in the way, Kat.' He'd had a bad experience with love too, but he was willing to make this work, put in the effort required and see how far it could go.

'Look,' he said, lowering his voice. 'This has moved past a fling for me—I…care about you.' The fearful look in her eyes made him shy away from confessing his true feelings. She was already looking at him as if she couldn't get away quickly enough. The L-bomb might scare her away for good.

'I care about you too, Nash.' She clenched her jaw as if her words were hard to get out. 'I also care about Molly. But she has everything she needs in you and Carol. I have to remember that Lucy only has me. *She* has to be my priority, irrespective of my feelings. I don't want us to let this go on longer and end up hurting the ones we love the most.'

Grady's blood turned to ice. 'So you're ending it, just like that?'

Obviously his feelings were very much one-sided. He'd rushed into this, despite lecturing himself on keeping things casual. He'd fallen for her and she still couldn't trust him, was unwilling to take a chance on him, preferring to keep herself closed-off, the way she'd done for six years after the last time she'd risked her heart. While he'd given his all, Kat might never be in a relationship place, not for him, anyway.

He sighed, the urge to beg rising up in his chest. 'I thought we were building something special here, Kat. I thought we might have a future together…you, me and our girls. Molly is already attached to you; I saw that last night.'

She nodded, her eyes bright with the sheen of

tears. 'Just as Lucy feels the same way for you.' Her expression was desolate.

Guilt shredded him; he was torn in so many directions.

'Don't you think that I've dreamed of a future with you?' she said, her voice strangled. 'But be honest—do you really see it working? The timing isn't right for either of us. There are so many things to consider, so many people's feelings at stake in order for us to be together.'

As if she'd made up her mind, she jutted out her chin with determination. 'I don't want to be hurt again, and I won't put Lucy through an emotional upheaval when it could all be for nothing. Molly has you *and* Carol to fall back on if it all went wrong. Lucy only has me. I have to be selfish for her sake.'

She was making it sound as if he and Carol were getting back together, one big happy family. Grady scrubbed a hand through his hair in confusion, aware that the clock was ticking and he needed to be on the ward five minutes ago.

'I told you I won't hurt you. I'm not your ex.' It was Kat he wanted. He understood that she was scared. He'd give her some space, and when Molly was recovered they could talk it all through.

Her face crumpled, her lip trembling. 'I know you would never intentionally hurt anyone,

Nash. You're a good man. But you and Carol and Molly—you'll always have each other, even if you and Carol aren't together, and I'm glad for you all. But if you and I didn't work out, and let's face it we can barely find time to conduct a fling, let alone anything more serious, I'd be alone again.'

Unable to argue with her logic, he faltered. He wanted to hold her and tell her it would all be okay, but she was right; his loyalties were as divided as his time. He needed to go upstairs to Molly. He couldn't even give Kat the time this conversation deserved.

As if sensing that she'd won her argument, Kat stiffened, stood taller, composed herself while he tensed for the blow he sensed was coming. 'I can't do that to Lucy. It's a risk I'm not willing to take. I'm sorry.'

She left his office and didn't look back.

CHAPTER SEVENTEEN

BY THE THIRD day after she'd ended things with
Nash, Kat's soul-searching had peaked. Heart-
sore and listless like a wrung-out dishcloth, she
fought the urge to call him on an hourly basis.
But she wanted to give him space; his priority
would be Molly, who was home from hospital.

And a call would only confirm that it was
over, something Kat's heart already knew.

Nash hadn't contacted her, despite the fact
that Molly was back at school, according to a
delighted Lucy. There had been no sign of him
at the hospital, his name blanked off the staff
roster for the rest of the week.

The distance had given Kat plenty of time
to think about the decision she'd made. He
was done with her, and she only had herself to
blame.

She'd been an utter coward, running scared
when she'd seen Nash and Carol and Molly together, when she'd heard him state that he didn't

want Carol back, the old doubts that she must be unworthy or unlovable because of Henry's rejection resurfacing with freshly sharpened claws. But what if she'd got it all wrong? What if, one day, he might want the same thing Kat dreamed of—their own family of four? Despite her feelings, she hadn't been able to trust him enough to overcome her fears, and she'd seen how that knowledge had hurt him.

To stave off the tears that hovered perilously close to the surface, Kat sipped her coffee, the ever-present lump of regret in her throat making it difficult to swallow.

I thought we might have a future together... you, me and our girls.

His brave and wonderful words from that fateful morning haunted her, threatening to set off the waterworks once more. But Kat refused to cry in front of Lucy, and she'd spent enough time this week locked in the bathroom with red and swollen eyes.

Of course his statement had given her hope. But when she'd tried to visualise the dream, to picture them happily living together under one roof, the sacrifices and complications—managing Carol's expectations, preparing their daughters to be sisters and stepdaughters, carving out enough 'them' time to make their relationship work—had overwhelmed her, blurring the vision like a swirl of paint in a jar of water.

Fear had taken hold. All Kat could see was the broken version of herself, the one hurt by another man.

How could *that* damaged and scared woman be everything Nash and Molly and Lucy needed?

'Mum, do you like my picture?' Lucy asked, startling Kat from her daunting ruminations. Lucy held up her drawing of what looked like a house and a family with two kids and a mum and dad.

A fresh wave of guilt slammed into the centre of Kat's chest. Perhaps, as Lucy grew older, a father figure, a whole family, would become increasingly important to her. Perhaps Kat had just been lucky up to that point, the questions about her daughter's missing parent few and far between.

Lucy's needs weren't reason enough for Kat to find a relationship, but in pushing Nash away she'd realised her biggest mistake yet—that *she* deserved to find happiness, to be a role model for her daughter, one who didn't give up on her dreams just because the journey was terrifying and hard.

'It's a lovely picture, darling,' she said, trying to avoid the panic that told her that this time she'd made the wrong choice in walking away.

Kat was so much more than the woman Henry had cast aside—alone and embittered, with no confidence in her own judgement. Kat and Lucy were as lovable as anyone else. Henry was the one with the problem. For his own messed-up reasons, he'd missed out on knowing his amazing little girl, more fool him.

'Tell me about your picture,' Kat said, pausing her reflections.

'That's the unquarium,' Lucy said with a smile, adorably mispronouncing the tricky word, 'and these are the penguins.' She pointed at some black blobs Kat had assumed were scribbles.

'And that's Nash and that's Molly next to you and me, Mum.'

Kat nodded, her eyes brimming that Lucy's version of a happy family included Nash and Molly. Kat wanted that too.

This time, she'd chosen a winner in Nash. She was brave enough to fall for a man worthy of her love. Just because she and Nash had each failed at relationships in the past didn't mean that they shouldn't give theirs a chance. What kind of a wimp would she be to allow fear of the unknown to dictate her happiness?

If she overcame that fear, the only thing stopping Kat from having her dream was the minor adjustments they would all need to make.

Reaching for her phone, Kat fired off a text to her babysitter.

She should have told him how she felt the last time she saw him, confessed that she was in love with him and agreed to do whatever it took to be together. She wasn't going to allow the sun to set on another day where she was too afraid to tell Nash how she felt.

'Come, on,' she said, placing the lids back on the marker pens Lucy had been using. 'Time for your bath and story and bed.'

Maybe she and Nash would work out, maybe they wouldn't, but there was only one way to find out, and the new fearless Kat deserved to know.

Grady locked his locker and tossed his scrubs into the used linen bin outside the staff changing rooms. Today had been his first shift back at work since Molly's discharge from hospital. Not only had he wanted to be around at home to ensure she'd fully recovered, a part of him had also been avoiding Kat. He'd deliberately put himself down for the late shift, knowing that she would have left Gulf Harbour by the time he started work.

It was a spineless thing to do, but until he'd fully processed their last conversation he didn't want to confront her and end up saying the wrong thing.

It's a risk I'm not willing to take.

Of course when she'd said that she'd meant that *he* was a risk not worth taking. Her words had winded him like a punch in the stomach. It was as if she didn't know him, didn't trust him at all, as if they were still those two strangers arguing over his rule-bending tendencies. But he was no longer the man who'd fancied her the minute she'd walked into the ER. That guy had been closed off to what he'd found with Kat since, and what he'd found was something real and rare. Something neither of them could afford to ignore, even though facing it was the harder option.

Just because circumstances had made him and Carol rush into marriage didn't mean he couldn't try again, nor did it mean that failure was inevitable, the way Kat seemed to suggest. Yes, there'd be hiccups along the way—there was in any relationship. Except Kat should realise by now that he'd do everything in his power for the women he loved—Molly, Kat and Lucy.

'Oh, you're still here—good.' Lauren stood in the doorway, snatching him away from a trip into fantasyland. 'I hoped I'd catch you.'

His friend's stare softened with sympathy. 'Is Molly still well?'

Grady nodded, smiled. 'She's all back to normal, running around, bossing her old man as usual.'

If only he could say that he was anywhere close to normal. He felt like a soft toy minus the stuffing. Because his normal would always be associated with Kat.

But he hadn't fought hard enough for her.

'So, what's up?' he said, hoping Lauren wasn't about to ask him to work late. He was tired, needed to call his parents and check on Molly.

'Nothing, really,' Lauren said. 'I just wondered when we can expect you back at work properly—I was hoping now that Molly's well you could resume your day shifts.'

He'd known Lauren a long time. They'd worked together for years. Her subtext was loud and clear: *You can't avoid Kat for ever.*

It wasn't a sustainable plan, mainly because if he didn't see her soon, tell her how he felt, he was going to explode.

She needed to know that he loved her and had everything all figured out. That last bit was a stretch, but he couldn't go on without her so they'd just have to make it work.

Frustrated, he shrugged into his jacket. 'As of today, I'm available for any shift you want.'

'Great.' Lauren grinned as if she could read the determination to win Kat over that was currently making his mind spin too fast.

Why had he allowed Kat's fear to trigger his own? So they were both scared to commit, scared to be hurt and resolved to protect their daughters. He'd show her that they could still do that and be together.

Eager to text Kat to meet him for breakfast tomorrow, he rushed past a smug Lauren. Then he paused, gripped her arms and placed a friendly kiss on her cheek.

'Thanks for the pep talk,' he said.

Forget breakfast tomorrow. He couldn't wait that long. He'd rush home, have a shower and call round to Kat's place tonight.

Bewildered but clearly delighted to see that he'd pulled himself together and come to his senses, Lauren laughed. 'You're welcome. Now, go get her, and don't come back to work until you've convinced her that you're the man of her dreams.'

Taking her sound advice, Grady sprinted to the hospital car park.

CHAPTER EIGHTEEN

KAT'S STOMACH TOOK another tumble as she stood on Nash's doorstep and sheltered from the rain. Inside, the house was dark, no sign that anyone was home. She should have called first, but the minute she'd acknowledged she'd made the wrong decision she'd wanted to see him, to say all of the things she'd bottled up inside since she'd started to develop feelings for him, which was some time after that very first kiss on his birthday.

Desperate, she pressed the doorbell once more, her teeth chattering, her feet soggy from running through the puddles on Nash's path and her sweater clinging to her damp skin. She pushed her wet hair back from her face; she must look a state. But none of that mattered.

She was about to dash around to the side of the house and peek through the windows when the front door flew open.

'Oh, you're home,' she said, her throat tight

with longing because Nash was naked but for the towel around his hips, his skin covered in water droplets like a sweating ice lolly on a scorching summer's day.

Kat licked her parched lips.

'I was in the shower,' he said, swinging the door wide, his shock fading. 'Come in. You're drenched.'

'It's raining,' she said, stating the obvious.

When Nash closed the door and faced her she almost lost her nerve. He was so gorgeous she wanted to throw herself into his arms. But she'd messed up, succumbed to her fear, hurt both him and herself in the process.

'Am I disturbing you?' she said, feeling sick with anticipation. Perhaps he was on his way out. Perhaps he had a date.

No matter. She'd come here to say her piece and say it she would.

'I was on my way to your place, actually. I just jumped in the shower after my shift.' His gaze traced her face, swept over her body, dousing Kat's chills in welcome heat. Perhaps it wasn't too late.

'Oh, good, because I think we should talk,' Kat said before she became too distracted by his bare chest. He was too far away. She wanted him all over her, but she wanted to tell him her feelings more.

'I agree.' He nodded, crossed his arms, looking far too relaxed and in command of his emotions whereas she was a trembling wreck.

'I've been thinking,' she continued, determined to be brave this time, 'and I've decided that you need to know how I feel. About us, about you.'

'I agree,' he said, his eyes burning bright into hers, stealing her breath.

'Is that all you're going to say?' she whispered because he was looking at her with such intensity it was hard to think. Or maybe there wasn't enough oxygen supplying her brain.

'No.' He dropped his arms and stepped closer, forcing Kat to look up at him. 'There's something new you should know about me.'

'There is?' She couldn't help but smile, even though her heart was in her mouth and they were yet to resolve a thing. She loved him. She loved every one of his revelations. Just standing here with him dripping was a precious gift.

'What is it?' she managed, her head spinning and knees weak.

'I love you, Kat,' he said, a triumphant smile on his face.

Kat gaped, her own declaration of love forgotten in the face of those amazing three little words.

'Wait…' She held up her palms, trying to control the rush of her emotions, which threatened to bowl her over.

'I'll wait as long as you need,' he said. 'But you have to know this.' He gripped her upper arms, grabbing her attention, although there was no need. Kat was engrossed in every word that came from his mouth. 'I wasn't thinking straight the last time we talked and now I am.'

She nodded, feeling the same, willing him to continue because she was so choked speech was impossible.

'I know you're scared.' His gaze softened. 'I am too. We've both been hurt and we're both protective of our girls. But I love you and I'm begging you to give us a chance.'

He loved her? Kat opened her mouth to speak, but still nothing.

'It doesn't have to happen overnight.' His hands slid to hers, gripping her fingers as if he'd never let her go. 'And obviously there will be lots of hurdles, but we can make this work. We have so much in common. We understand the pressures of each other's work. We're both family-orientated, and I love you. I might have already mentioned that.'

His vulnerable smile was her undoing. She nodded, tears pricking the backs of her eyes.

Misinterpreting her continued muteness, he stepped closer and cupped her face. 'Please give us a chance at a relationship, Kat. You and I deserve happiness as much as our girls. If we're content, they can only benefit. We can take it slow... I promise. Date properly for a while, and when we think the time is right, when we think they might be ready, we can explain it to the girls, prepare them for us to become a family, living together.'

Kat snapped out of her daze. Her joy was too much. He was describing every one of the dreams she'd dared to believe possible. 'Nash...'

But he seemed to be caught up in his enthusiasm, his speech still persuasive, emerging in a rush. 'I've already told Carol that I'm in love with you, not that it's anything to do with her, but we're all going to have to get along for Molly's sake. But I swear that you and our girls are my priority. We'll always do what's right for the four of us. Just please say you'll give us a chance to do it together.'

Impatient, Kat tugged on his hands. 'Nash, can you let me get a word in, please, before you make up all of the rules on your own?'

He swallowed, contrite and nervous-looking. 'Of course, sorry. I've just had all of that bottled inside for so long. Okay, you go.'

'Thank you.' She sighed, expelling her relief and elation in one big shudder. Before he could list ten more reasons why she should give them a chance, she stood on tiptoes and kissed him, pulling back quickly to reassure him that she'd heard every word he'd said and felt the same.

'I love you too, Nash. I came over to tell you because I didn't want you to give up on us, the way I stupidly did the day Molly was discharged. You're right, I was scared. I overheard you and Carol talking and I freaked out. But meeting you, knowing you, has made me strong enough to be open to love again. You're the best man I've ever met.' She stepped into the circle of his arms and gripped his face in both hands. 'You're a wonderful father, a brilliant nurse and don't even get me started on your prowess as a lover.'

He smiled, his arms around her waist a little tighter.

'I was overwhelmed when I realised how much you and Molly mean to me,' she said, needing to explain why she'd messed up, that it had nothing to do with her feelings for the two of them. 'I didn't mean what I said. You *are* worth the risk. You're worth any risk. I know that there are no guarantees in life, but I don't need them, Nash. I just need you and Molly and me and Lucy. I just need us.'

With a groan, Nash hauled her close and brought his mouth down on top of hers, his kiss hard and passionate and full of the love they'd just declared.

In the frantic embrace that followed, where they kissed and laughed and kissed some more, his towel slipped from his hips and fell to the floor.

'I love you so much,' he said, staring deep into her eyes. 'I want so many things for us, but I mean it; we can take it slow. I won't bombard you with proposals here and now, especially as I'm completely naked.'

Kat laughed, part of her wanting to hear those proposals. But he was right. They needed to consider what was best for all four of them before they rushed ahead, carried away by the emotions that for so long Kat had cast aside.

She slid her hands up his back, nuzzled her face against his chest. 'I should probably get out of these wet things myself.' He was hard against her stomach. She surrendered to the temptation she'd fought since the minute he'd opened the door and licked a stray water droplet from his skin.

'It would be a shame to waste such a golden opportunity...' she raised her eyes to his '...don't you think?'

Nash grinned, scooped her up in his arms and strode towards the bedroom.

'Whatever you say.' He kissed her, laying her

down on the bed. 'You make the rules and I'll follow.'

'Oh, I like the sound of that,' she said, laughing as Nash stripped away her clothes.

Soon, with his every touch reverent, his kisses showing Kat the truth of all his declarations, there was no space for anything other than the love they both deserved.

EPILOGUE

Kat sifted the warm golden sand through the sieve of her fingers, one eye on Lucy and Molly frolicking in the sea a short distance away. The low, late afternoon sun glinted off the water, temporarily blinding her, but she wasn't concerned. She knew that Nash too would be watching their girls play, ensuring that they didn't wander out too deep.

He shifted, adjusting her head where she lay on his lap, his fingers stroking through the strands of her hair as if he needed to ensure she was real, to constantly touch her, to connect.

The feeling was mutual.

In the two months that they'd been an official couple the four of them had been virtually inseparable. A blended family. Complete.

Kat's rules and schedules had helped to keep everyone on track at all times—appointments kept, deadlines met, childcare juggled—and Nash's easygoing patience meant that even at the most hectic moments there was always time for a giggle, a hug or a passionate kiss.

'Am I squashing you?' she asked, turning her face away from the water's edge to look up at her gorgeous man with a smug grin.

'No.' He took her hand and raised it to his lips, kissing her knuckles. 'And even if you were I wouldn't care.'

Kat smiled, so content she almost felt guilty. She had a wonderful partner, their daughters were still the best of friends, and she'd even just passed her trauma exams.

Life was perfect.

'I've been thinking,' Nash said, his gaze flitting from her to Lucy and Molly and then back again, 'about Christmas presents. Why don't the girls just share a trampoline? They're pretty much always together anyway.'

Confused, Kat sat up. 'But Molly already has a trampoline… Why would you buy her another one?'

Nash tilted his head, his grin wide and his stare indulgent as if waiting for her to catch up.

'I'm asking you and Lucy to move in with us, Kat.'

Kat froze, her mind tripping over itself in her haste to comprehend. But there was no time for her usual overthinking, a wave of love rushing in to obliterate everything in its path.

'Do you think they're ready?' Her *yes* hovered on her lips, no deliberation required.

Lucy and Molly were at the centre of every decision they made, whether it was a trip to the beach or the *sleepovers* they'd tentatively trialed for the past two weekends, where the girls had shared the bunk beds in Molly's room and Kat had ostensibly stayed in the spare room for appearance's sake, only sneaking into Nash's bed when the girls were out for the count.

'I think they'll take it in their stride,' Nash said, once more checking on the girls. 'Just like they accepted that sometimes Lucy's mum and Molly's dad kiss each other.'

Kat's blood heated at the expression on his face. 'Well, Lucy's mum fancies the pants off Molly's dad.' She leaned into his side, shoulder to shoulder, tilting her face up for a relatively chaste kiss.

She couldn't ravage him on a public beach, but later, when the girls were asleep, all bets were off.

'So is that a yes?' he whispered against her lips when she reluctantly pulled back. 'Will you move in with us? I want to wake up with you in my arms. I want to be lulled asleep by your heartbeat against my chest. I want to live with you for the rest of my life.'

The prickle of tears threatened. Kat pressed

her mouth once more to his, awash with love for the man who'd made her and Lucy's life complete. 'Yes.'

His smile widened. 'Good. In that case, it's time for today's new Nash fact. Now that we're going to be living together, it will make much more sense.'

Kat laughed, giving him a playful shove. 'You're not going to tell me that you leave the toilet seat up are you, because that I already know.'

Nash's expression grew serious, his eyes brimming with the love that wrapped around Kat like a safety net.

'Are you ready?'

She nodded, captivated by the intensity in his eyes.

He gripped her fingers, his thumb swiping across the back of her hand. 'I'll love you for ever, Kat.'

She was about to say he'd told her that last week and the week before, but he shushed her, placed his fingertips against her lips.

'Which is why, in about ten seconds,' he said, dragging out the suspense, 'I'm going to ask you to marry me.'

She wasn't sure how he'd managed to render her utterly speechless again, but it didn't matter. Sometimes actions spoke louder than words, and Nash had been showing her that he was a man she could rely on from the first day they'd met.

She leaned into him, kissed him, clung to him, determined to never let him go for as long as they lived.

'So will you?' he said, laughing when she let him up for air.

'Yes, yes, I will,' she said, laughing too, tears in her eyes. Spying the girls running up from the sea towards them in her peripheral vision, she stole one last kiss.

'Good decision,' he said, falling back against the sand good-naturedly as he was attacked by two giggling five-year-olds.

Yes, perfect decision, thought Kat, joining the tumble.

* * * * *

*If you missed the previous story in the
Gulf Harbor ER duet, then check out*

Tempted by the Rebel Surgeon

*If you enjoyed this story, check out
these other great reads from
JC Harroway*

How to Resist the Single Dad
Forbidden Fling with Dr. Right
Tempting the Enemy

All available now!